# FIRST FLIGHT

# FIRST FLIGHT

## J.R. DANIELS

Coward, McCann & Geoghegan
New York

# ◢ 1 ◣

A lot of nonsense is talked about first flights. Some of it is ignorance; the rest is a mystique built up by the public relations boys for onward transmission by their friends from the papers. For a design team, there is much less high drama about a first flight, more a feeling of relief at being able to tick an important stage off the development programme. Once the ground checks are complete and the taxi runs have gone as far as runway length allows, the first flight follows easily, naturally. There was no reason why the Morland President should have been any exception.

Morlands themselves were an exception; in no way demonstrative, but dour in true Yorkshire tradition. There was no turn-out of the works, no great line-up of spectators to see the President airborne. The only men watching were those with something to learn, or contribute. Those few, the design team leaders, had stretched their lunch into the early afternoon, knowing that John Rose would not take off until he had the best possible visibility. With the wind from the east rolling back the industrial haze, it was getting better all the time. It was like that for six months of the year; later on the haze would creep back, as the wind dropped during the early evening.

The President actually went at ten to three, sliding into the air as though she knew it was her natural element, rotating easily into the climb. Even when the reheat was cut she went on accelerating visibly, slanting for the cloud gaps.

5

'She's even noisier than we thought,' said somebody, clearly impressed.

'Give us time,' said the powerplant engineer. 'If you'd *wanted* a three month hold, we could've taken five decibels off the sideline.' She was almost gone, but they could still hear the roar.

So could the others. They, the unofficial spectators, more or less interested, looked up and saw the President for the first time; looked for a big aeroplane because of the noise, and were disappointed. They saw ninety feet of slender fuselage borne by fifty feet of razor-blade wing, balanced by a foreplane, carried along by two massive underslung jets. It was a new sky-shape they could make little sense of, and that was how Morlands wanted it.

All went well for the full scheduled hour. The team in the control tower looked and listened. The radar plot, the telemeter traces, above all the calm voice of their Chief Test Pilot, all built up a picture for the skilled observers. Mentally, they plotted the corners of the first flight envelope.

In coming back she passed directly over the field, orbiting gently left, easing down from five thousand. The afternoon had cleared nicely, though the sun was low and orange. The President's take-off had been over the plain to the east, so the approach brought her close over the town to the west. A feeble ray of sun caught her as she turned from the downwind leg. Even at that distance they heard the throttles opened to hold the speed as the wheels and flaps came down. John Rose had established a loose circuit to give himself some scope, just in case.

It is always the last mile of the approach, the actual touchdown which carries the best chance of something going wrong. The lower you come, and the slower you go, the tighter the margins become, and it doesn't matter whether you are on your first solo or a top industry test pilot. It didn't seem to worry the President. She turned finals away over the town, as though dodging the streamers of mill smoke, and settled on the approach.

Afterwards, they argued who sensed it first. The anxiety spread through them like a slow ripple; it was perhaps

6

half a minute before they could all see it. The President was getting too high on the approach; too high and too slow. Twin trails of smoke came from the engines as the throttles were opened wide. Then the roar of the reheat hit them, and they knew something was far wrong.

'He's going round again.'

'Shut up.' The tension snapped back into place.

'...can't *hold* her...' The voice, almost as if in agony, came through the loudspeaker.

They could all see that. It was too late for the engines to help. The President was already too slow, the nose too high. Full power served only to push her steeper into the fatal climb, so that she rose above the plain, her full planform clear against the lowering sun. For a moment she seemed to hang, balanced on the jets. Sheer thrust kept her there, near-vertical, but could not do it for ever. She fell away on one wing as though a giant hand had cut a string, and the burnished silver shape whipped through half a turn of spin and vanished behind the jumbled roofs of the Old Works.

Nobody moved. They all knew what it meant and many of them had seen it before, but they did no more than wince as they sensed the impact, and stare at the upward-bursting mushroom cloud. There is something riveting about a crash. One stands and imagines the aircraft as it was, a few seconds before, still airborne.

The emergency services were better drilled. By the time the sound of the explosion reached them, perhaps ten seconds later, the fire engines and ambulances were on their way.

'Christ,' came a voice, 'why the hurry? It's a dustpan and brush job, that.'

They found the crudity embarrassing. Sir William Morland himself detailed off those with an immediate interest, and led a general exodus from the control tower. A nervous little group trailed him back to the headquarters building. It was not only the engineers who were dreaming up questions, and not liking the answers.

7

# ◢2◣

It was a bad morning. That was nothing new; they mostly were nowadays. I had Liz to thank for that. It was supposed to be above clock-watching, our office, but I couldn't remember the last time I hadn't been late. They were bound to start in on me sooner or later. What the hell; if they did, I would tell them to take a running jump. Liz was banking on me doing it sometime soon. It was her money that would give me the chance.

Tony didn't so much as give me time to settle down and make sure I was awake. He hauled me in, fed me a coffee and a morning paper, and waited for a reaction. Tony was fair: he wouldn't have given me anything without good reason, not even the bawling-out I was half expecting, so I sank the coffee and looked at the front page.

Half of it was taken up with an air-to-ground shot; a hole in a railway line with half an aeroplane sticking out of it. I didn't recognise the aeroplane, which worried me more than it would have worried most people, but then aeroplanes are my job. I skimmed past the two-inch letters which said Secret Wonder Plane Crashes and looked for some facts. They were notable for their absence. Then I came to the name Morlands and stopped reading, because I didn't want to know about another name chopped from my dwindling list of friends. Tony saw me freeze and jerked the hook while I was still on it.

'Didn't you know John Rose pretty well?'

I skimmed the rest of the column. 'It doesn't say it was John.'

'It doesn't say so. But it was.'

I looked at him with an effort. 'John was on squadron

with me,' I said. 'We went through ETPS together. He was best man when I married Liz. He pulled me out of a burning aeroplane at Boscombe. All of which you know; so what are you leading up to?'

'We all lose friends from time to time.' It was skilled use of the needle, waking me up by degrees, but fast.

'I'm surprised you've any to lose. Just get on with it, please.'

He framed another crack and thought better of it. 'British Rail are cross,' he said. I knew that if I looked blank he would carry on. It would be quicker that way.

'That's the main Leeds-London line you're looking at. They only just stopped an express in time. Now they're having to send everything round via York.'

'Wait a minute.' I was trying to piece it together. 'There's been nothing about a new Morlands aircraft.'

'No, indeed.'

'But it *is* new, Tony, isn't it? I mean, I don't recognise it.' I studied the picture more carefully. 'It's pretty big, and obviously high performance, yet we've not had so much as a whisper of it. What are they playing at?'

'At the moment, they're playing poker, with their cards close to their chest and the press on the other side of the table.'

I stared at him, and light dawned. Morlands' security had been really tight. There was no telling why, but commercial secrets are taken much more seriously than national ones except at the very highest level. Their aircraft had crashed, and no doubt the company would have clammed up on the whole thing had they been given the chance. Coroner's court, confidential affidavits, a word to the Ministry and nobody would be much the wiser.

But Morlands hadn't been given the chance. You don't chop a hole in a main railway line, close to a centre of population, without creating a lot of interest. Right now, they would be fending off some very awkward questions and wondering how to deal with the aftermath.

'Don't tell me they want to drag *us* into it.'

'You can still be bright when you feel like it.' That was a point Tony was entitled to score.

9

'It's hardly fair. They've told us absolutely nothing, and now they expect us to go and help them sort it out.' It was obvious, really. The legal situation following the loss of a manufacturer's private-venture prototype is complicated. The manufacturer has plenty of opportunity to drag his heels and plead commercial security. But if Morlands didn't ask us, the Accident Investigation Branch, for help, the newspaper and radio people would have a field day with them, and they would just be the front of the queue.

'I don't know how much they'll tell us, even now.' Tony was half engineer, half politician; essential qualifications for any department head.

I blinked at him. 'You mean they want us in, but only for the sake of appearances?'

'That's right. Consider yourself elected.'

We were invited, as long as we didn't overstep the mark; tricky. 'Me?' I said.

'You're the right man for this job.'

'Come *on*, Tony. You need someone tactful and disinterested. I'm ruled out on either count.'

'Now there I agree with you.' He smiled for the first time. 'Nevertheless, it's yours. By request.'

'Whose request?'

'My masters at the Ministry.'

'We're autonomous. Tell them to get lost.'

'Not without good reason.'

'I'm a good reason, aren't I?' He knew my history, he knew Liz, he knew better than anyone the decline in my work over the last year.

'They were very insistent. I think I'll go along with them.' He leaned forward over his desk. 'Listen. If this was an ordinary job, you'd be about last on the list. But it's not ordinary. Most of my officers would go up there and play it straight. Well, I'm damned if we're going into business as a sort of glorified public relations firm for the industry when it wants pulling out of trouble. You're insubordinate and irresponsible; try it on old Morland.'

'*He* didn't ask for me.'

'No. But he'll have asked the Minister for the right man.'

'The Minister's not as up to date on me as you are.'

'Right. So bear this in mind, too; step out of line and I'll throw you out, and be glad to.'

'Thanks very much. I'm going up to read the riot act to Morlands, but if I step out of line I'm fired. It would serve you right if I was a good boy and did whatever Morlands told me to do.'

'Neil,' he said, with an air of slight pleading. 'I don't know how your name came up, or why. I'm not concerned with other people's motives...'

'I'm not surprised. Your own are twisted enough to keep most people going.'

'For goodness' sake!' I had goaded him into half-anger. 'We are here to investigate accidents, and you're going to investigate this one. While you're about it you'll have to stall not only the press and the local authorities, but Morlands as well. I can't tell you to play it straight because it's not a straight sort of job. You're on your own, and you'll have to be unorthodox: your personal interest may set you digging deep enough to find all the pieces. Morlands will humour you to keep you on their side; you could turn that to advantage.'

He must have been thinking about it all night.

# ◢3◣

Twenty-four hours later, the trains were still going round via York, though progress was being made at the site of the crash. It's an acquired art, taking a mental photograph as you fly over something, but it had been part of my later education.

I could see that most of the wreckage had gone, though the digging teams were still at work. The crash had taken out all four lines; on either side of the crater, the railway engineers were ready and waiting with their equipment.

The crater was barely a mile from the runway threshold, displaced some hundred yards to the left. That was easy enough to judge, for I passed it on my own approach to the same runway. Morlands' airfield was quite a place, snuggling between the industrial towns, half-hidden beneath the morning haze, reputedly boasting the worst visibility record of any major field in the country. It wasn't even the biggest scar on the much-scarred local landscape: perhaps that was why it had lasted so long. The coal-tips rose round it, the two great motorways hemmed it in to west and north, and the twin east-west runways, one old and short and the other new and very long, had been ruled across ravaged moorland, fitting the scene to perfection.

I eased the Cherokee to a smooth touchdown, trying harder than usual, for I still had my pride. The control tower returned the compliment by turning me left on to one of the main aprons, and they gave me the full marshaller-and-groundcrew treatment. I watched them top off the tanks and push the aircraft towards a big hangar, and by that time George Simpson had arrived.

Sometimes you can tell how things are going to go by who they send to meet you. In that respect Simpson was neutral; a brisk fifty, hair still dark, dress sense good. He had a well-polished Rover and a smile to match; he was Morlands' head of security. There was no point in taking it as a calculated insult. In a firm Morlands' size—and with their special problems—the security chief is no retired country copper. I put Simpson down as an ex-MI honours graduate, an expert on internal problems, industrial espionage and Ministry security alike.

'Funny, really,' he said as we drove away. 'Until we had your signal we never imagined you flying up. Nice little aeroplane, your own, is it? Not Ministry issue, I imagine.'

'My wife's,' I said with disarming honesty. 'But I fly it.'

He left it at that and filled me in on the details as we

cruised round the perimeter track. By the time we had crossed to the south side of the airfield I had a layman's view of the crash itself, and an expert summary of all subsequent action. He didn't try to paint over the problems. British Rail understandably wanted their line open again, and the hell with taking a week to sift the plot and salvage the last vestiges of wreckage. The locals were divided between those with a straightforward morbid interest, and those who wanted all flying stopped in case the next one fell on them. The local authorities were wondering whether to back them up, the police were complaining about lack of co-operation and the strain on their manpower, and the press were present in force. Morlands were doing their best to conduct a holding operation with them all.

Simpson told me this as we made our way across the airfield, stopping every so often to check with the tower before carrying on. Strangely, perhaps, I had never been there before, and the whole place made a profound impression on me. It came in three parts. I had landed on North Field with its long runway, big aprons and modern overhaul and flight sheds. Then we crossed a single-track mineral railway and came to South Field which had been the centre of Morlands' activity during the last war; away to our right, much nearer the town, slumbered the jumble of the Old Works, which had been their factory in the war before that. Finally we crossed a main railway line and found ourselves in South Works, the massive main factory which nowadays carried the bulk of the production work.

Then we moved out of the factory gate, along a public road, and the headquarters building loomed in front of us.

# 4

It was a typical modern mausoleum, except that it was not as high as most. It was too close to the approach path for that. But it would have looked more in place in central London than on the edge of the Yorkshire moors. Perhaps, I thought, that was Morlands' strength and also in a way their weakness; they had no London office. If you wanted to see them, you came up here to Barnsdale where they were registered. If you came with good reason—with hard cash and a need for good aeroplanes—people reckoned they did you well. Otherwise, you were in for a hard time. So they said, and I had never sought to prove otherwise, until now.

Sir William Morland had his office on the top floor. It was a big, uncomfortable room, sparsely furnished, dimly decorated; yet I was to find that he spent much of his time in it. There was nothing of aviation about it, no models or pictures, no awards for achievement—though Morland aircraft had achieved plenty. It was a room that summed up a whole mental attitude, one which had no time for frivolity. There was only one picture, that of old Sir Arthur Morland, who had built up the firm through one war and turned it into a colossus during the next. Somewhere I had heard that Sir William's son had been christened Arthur, after his illustrious grandfather.

I stood uneasily in this sanctum of a puritanical industrialist, who fitted it no less well than his father might have done, and his gaze never left me.

'Thank you, Simpson,' he said, and George took his cue and slid out without another word.

'So you're Goddard.' The pale blue eyes clashed with the dark brown hair, through which the grey pushed round

14

the edges. Sir William Morland was a big man, bigger even than me.

'Yes, sir.' I tried to keep it neutral, and found myself wondering whether it had slid off into insolence or subservience.

He picked up a slender file from his desk, opened it, but did not look down. 'You know something about crashes, do you not?' The Yorkshire was strong in his voice. Old Sir Arthur had spent his brass on a sound school, but not a posh one.

'I'm as well qualified as most.'

'You're a bloody sight better qualified than most. Been up the sharp end of one or two, hast thou not?'

'If you know that, you'll not need telling about them, will you?' I was annoyed to find myself slipping into his northern phraseology.

'Doesn't follow, lad.' His eyes narrowed, and I fancied he had a keen ear. 'They've not told me everything here.'

'I wouldn't have thought George Simpson was a man to leave things out.'

'Bloody Simpson.' Unfairly, he dismissed the competence of his security chief with a dialect sweep of the tongue. 'He'll not tell me what *sort* of man you are.'

'You'll have to be your own judge of that.' I wanted to make him as annoyed as he was making me.

'I usually am.' He glowered at me as though daring me to push him any harder. 'But I was given no time. You've been wished on me, Goddard. You're a political appointee. I told Barry Mayhew I wanted someone who'd keep the press happy and his nose out of trouble. Why the bloody hell'd he send you?'

Sir Barrington Mayhew was Minister for Aerospace.

'You tell me.' It made me think, hard. I had been somebody's choice. But whose, and why?

'I wish I could.' He thumped the file. 'This says you're an imminent disaster.'

'All right,' I said, 'I'll go back and tell them. They'll have somebody else up here in a day or two. You'll have to handle the press on your own until then.'

'Don't be bloody daft!' He almost shouted, then dropped his voice low. 'I've not the time to throw you back, Goddard. *This* is crisis day. You're going to be something of a front man. What sort of a front man are you going to make?'

'Front man? There was nothing in my briefing about holding your PRO's hand.'

'Stuff your briefing.' He hovered between impatience and venom. 'You'll help keep these people off our backs, and you'll be given sufficient technical background to make a good job of it.' I opened my mouth to reply, and he chopped me off by abruptly switching tack. 'You worry me,' he said. 'Why does a successful test pilot suddenly chuck it up, get a job in AIB and take to pottering about in a bloody little Piper?'

'Because I crunched a Goshawk at Boscombe.'

'You look fit enough to me.'

'I'm fit enough. I gave it up, that's all.'

'It's not all. Lose your nerve, did you?' His voice was empty of implication.

'No. My wife lost hers.'

'That's a new one. Never knew it stop a man flying before, not if he wanted to carry on.'

'Her father died in a crash. She was an only child; they were very close.' I wondered if he had *that* in his confounded file. 'Six months later she nearly lost me in another crash. She's not to be blamed for caving in.'

'You don't blame her, I take it?' He stared at me for a long moment and let his eye fall to the file for the first time. 'Married, 1966, Elizabeth, daughter of Sir Andrew Wallace.' It came out flat, impersonal. 'Did all right for yourself, didn't you?'

'So did you,' I said rudely. It was well enough known that old Sir Arthur had pushed William into a dynastic match with the daughter of another Yorkshire industrialist.

He simply nodded, but his eyes sparkled a warning. 'Andrew died in that messy Nairobi crash, did he not?' The way he dropped into easy first-name terms with my deceased father-in-law underlined his air of menace.

'If I hadn't given up test flying, Liz would have ended up in a mental home,' I said. 'The AIB seemed the next best thing.'

'But you didn't really need a job, did you?' He unbalanced me with his intelligence. 'Andrew left a tidy packet; more than I shall. Can't blame a tax expert for that. You must be doing well enough without poking around in other people's misfortunes.'

'I could still take umbrage and go back to London,' I warned. 'You know the answer to that one.'

'Don't take on so, lad.' He gave a humourless grin. 'I wanted to see if *you* knew the answer. I'd rather have no man at all than the wrong one. Listen,' he said earnestly, 'I'm not an aeroplane man, Goddard. I'm a people man. A money man. I said I needed to know what sort of man you were.' He let it sink in. 'What are you? You're a poor man with a rich wife. You want to stand on your own feet and you have to fight her to do it. What's more, you knew John Rose. You could be a strength or a weakness.'

'What's it to you? I'm not on your staff.'

'Only because it wouldn't be politic to pay you.'

'You can do better than that.' He had gone too far to be serious, I hoped.

'Don't be bloody impertinent.' He said it without heat. 'If you can take that much and keep your head, you'll not do badly up here.'

'You cunning old bastard.' It formed and slipped out before I could stop it.

'If you ever call me that again,' Morland warned, 'I'll have your hide. Right though you may be,' he added as an afterthought. Some of the tension evaporated.

'Normally,' I said, thinking of Tony's instructions, 'the Ministry would have a fit at the idea of one of its officers shooting off his mouth without reference to higher authority. You say it's the whole idea of my being up here. Fair enough; it fits in with some ideas of my own. But if I'm to back you up, I want something in return.'

'You'll not blackmail me.' Morland tipped his head on one side and narrowed his eyes.

'Call it that if you like. I want to play a full part—a *full* part,' I stressed, 'in this investigation.'

'We're capable of sorting this thing out by ourselves, Goddard, without AIB peering over our shoulders. What's your worry? As long as you play it straight, I'll see you get the credit. It's something I deny my own back room boys.'

'Stuff the credit.' I borrowed his own vulgarism.

'What, then?' Morland was very much on his guard.

'I have to do a proper job. I can't convince the news boys it's all under control unless I'm convinced myself. And I'll not take anyone's unsupported word for that, however bright he is.'

'It's not on, lad. Keep thy nose where it belongs.' Each word came down like a sledgehammer.

'Just what are you afraid of?' I couldn't let him dig his heels in like that. 'What is this aeroplane, anyway? You built and flew it without a murmur getting out, not even to us. It's big and high-performance, so it must have cost millions. Is that the trouble? Is the whole issue so dodgy that you'd keep it away from anybody who's not under your direct control?'

He didn't answer at once, but stared out of the big picture window. It faced south across the moors, I saw, and gave no view of the airfield.

'Did you know your father-in-law well?' he asked eventually.

'Not really.' The change of subject worried me. What was Morland leading up to? 'He wasn't much of a character,' I explained. 'And he· wasn't around very long after I arrived on the scene.'

'You do him less than justice, lad. He was a fine brain. Picked away until he'd come to the fundamentals. I wondered if you'd known him long enough to pick up the technique.'

'No. It's all mine.'

'You listen to me.' He swung round in a moment of genuine anger. 'It's no time for clever answers off the cuff. If I let you in on this, you'll soon enough be in a position to break Morlands. No,' he said as I opened my mouth to speak, 'I mean that. You say you can't do a decent job without knowing it all, but there's more to it than that. Why do you want to know? What makes you push so hard?'

'But you're going to let me in,' I said flatly, 'or you wouldn't even have told me that.'

'I'm going to let you in.' He hesitated. 'It's my own judgement, mind; I'm seldom wrong. Maybe you want it for John's sake. Maybe you want to climb back into the world and away from Elizabeth Wallace; whatever your reason, I judge it's a right one. No man's infallible, I could be wrong; you could break us. If you do, I'll break you, lad. You know I can.'

'Yes,' I said. 'I know.'

'Right, then. I've not the time nor the technical mind to explain to you. Go with Simpson, find your hotel and have lunch. By the time you're back, I'll have a team waiting to give you the background. Late this afternoon there's a press conference. Coroner's preliminary hearing the day after tomorrow; just a bit of chatter and an adjournment. You'll be on hand for all that.'

'Just to keep them happy.'

'Get your chip off your bloody shoulder. You've got what you wanted, have you not?' He was angry again. 'You're the man from the Ministry. You've one thing none of us have; respectability. For pity's sake hang on to it.'

I wondered what he meant by that.

# ◢5◣

'President,' said Ray Brooks, 'was built for an unfulfilled need, like all our aircraft.' Brooks was Morlands' Sales Director. His was the job of spotting such needs.

'In essence,' he said as the first slide flashed up, 'it's a small supersonic airliner. Not a commercial proposition in the airline sense, you must understand that. But Concorde is still some way off, isn't it? And in the meantime, there are plenty of people—heads of state, top civil servants, captains of industry—to whom time is money; lots of money. In the most extreme cases, it can be literally priceless.'

'A supersonic executive jet.' I tried to pull him down a peg, but he wouldn't have it.

'Too big for that. It has twenty-five seats.'

'That's a lot of top people.'

'Not really. *Top* people,' said Brooks with a verbal bow in their direction, 'travel with an entourage. Luggage. Their own communications gear.'

'Besides,' came another voice, 'we couldn't make it any smaller.' This was Brian Bates, the brain behind the President and Morlands' Chief Designer. The salesman grimaced, but Bates ploughed on. 'You have to give *top* people room to stand up inside. Put some structure round them, you've got a seven-foot diameter fuselage. To get a good supersonic fineness ratio, say twelve to one, the thing comes out ninety feet long. Fill the middle bit with fuel, baggage hold in the tail, you've still the room for twenty-odd seats. But don't expect Ray to tell you it's owt but a virtue.' Like Morland himself, unlike Brooks, the Chief Designer was Yorkshire.

'He has a point,' Brooks came back smoothly. 'It's as small as we can make it, but why worry? It's just right for my customers.'

'Customers? You've actually tried to sell it?' The shape on the screen had a certain rightness about it. It grew on me.

'We've canvassed the idea in one or two places, very discreetly. It's not the kind of thing we'd fancy anyone else having a go at. The market wouldn't take competition.'

'It looks a pretty simple aeroplane, considering,' I ventured. It had straight wings each with a single engine slung beneath.

'Simple means cheap,' said Brooks. 'Cheap to build, cheap to maintain. That's the hub of its appeal. That, and the speed.'

'But,' I argued, 'you'll never get a competitive lift-drag ratio with a shape like that.'

'You've lost track of the argument already,' said Bates. 'It doesn't *need* to be competitive in that sense. Our market won't worry about an extra fifty dollars a passenger on the cost of an Atlantic crossing.'

'As he says.' Brooks didn't sound too happy at having a technical man make the points for him.

'Look at it this way.' Bates pressed on regardless. They didn't love one another, these two, however much each respected the other. 'We started out with a sort of miniature Concorde, and scared ourselves witless with the cost and the timescale.'

'And the aerodynamics,' I suggested.

'Oh no.' Bates was quick to jump on that one. 'Morlands is never scared by technical problems, we can hold our own with anybody. No; it was just plain wrong. If you try scaling down Concorde, you end up with an abortion, because the engines end up too big for the rest of it. Besides, we were very worried about field performance as well as development time. Then we realised we were barking up the wrong tree. In the end we cleared the drawing board and stuck down a tube of fuselage, and a wing, and two bloody great engines.'

'Only two engines? That must give you some problems if you lose one.'

'Not at all. As I said, field performance is very important to us...'

'No point in being tied down to international airports,' Brooks interrupted. 'Much better if we can get into anything reasonable. Not a dirt strip, that would be ridiculous, but any six-thousand-foot hard runway, yes.'

'That's right.' Bates took it up smoothly. 'To get it out of that sort of field, there's only one answer: sheer power. Hence the ruddy great engines. They're reheat turbofans, by the way, which gets us back some of that Concorde margin.'

'I see.' He was right; they were ruddy great engines. I scaled them off the slide; if the fuselage was ninety feet long, the engine pods were well over twenty. 'Plenty of power, so she keeps on going when one goes out.'

'Right.' Bates was warming to his lecture. 'Now, see how

it all fits together? Once we were out of the mental strait-jacket, it all made sense. By having a straight wing, we could do many things at once. First, it was easy to design, almost a simple scaling-up job. Second, we could stick on the whole catalogue of high-lift devices, so as to get *into* that six-thousand-foot field. Leading edge slats; blown flaps; you name it, the President has it.'

'What else?' I prodded.

'Third; we sling the engines underneath. Very good from a structure point of view, and it can help the aerodynamics too. The engines are close to the ground, very easy to work on, even to change if need be. They're also widely separated, so if one engine blows up it doesn't wreck the other.'

'But the main thing,' came Brooks' smooth interjection, 'is that by doing it this way, we could do it quick and cheap.'

'Did you think of putting the engines back at the tail?' Bates' technical command fascinated the engineer in me.

'Of course we did. There's almost nothing to be said for it, once you look carefully, except for easier control if an engine fails. Against that you have a heavier structure, more complicated fuel and flap blowing systems, no room for an auxiliary power unit, and the engines sit in the wing wake at high incidence.' The way he said it, I knew he hadn't run out of reasons.

'Why the foreplane?' I asked, for instead of a conventional tailplane the President had a pair of all moving surfaces just aft of the pilot's cabin.

'Mainly to help with the field performance,' said Bates. 'With the foreplane, we add lift instead of subtracting it on the approach where the aeroplane is set in a nose-high attitude. Apart from that, the engineering is easy; a nice short control run instead of a nightmare running the whole length of the fuselage. The gust response is poor, of course, but that's hardly the worry for the President that it would be for a low-level combat aircraft.'

'You make it sound lovely. Can I order one now?'

'Can I have your cheque for two million?' The smooth counter came inevitably from Brooks.

'And how many easy payments?'

'None. Just two million.'

'You're joking.' Two million was folding money for most people, but for the President it was dirt cheap. They were talking about Concorde costing eight times as much, to carry six times as many people; and without writing off the development costs.

'Two million.' Brooks caught my mood exactly. 'That's writing off the development costs over a run of a hundred.'

'It makes no sense,' I protested. 'Why so much secrecy? The Americans could never touch you at that price?'

'Maybe not.' He became very serious. 'But they could have a stab at it, and maybe beat us on development time. That's why we elected to keep it very dark, maintaining our lead as long as possible. We also decided to telescope the actual development as much as possible. I'll admit there was another aspect of the secrecy angle, since you're supposed to be on our side. It's not going to be a popular aeroplane with the environment lobby. Not to mention its being the greatest status symbol ever.'

'Oh, sure.' We could all take that as read. 'But the *main* reason is to avoid giving anyone else the idea. What was all that about telescoping the development time? You'll have to argue that one with the ARB.' Because anyone can build and fly an aeroplane without reference to anyone, as long as they are an Air Registration Board approved design organisation (the trick is to gain ARB approval). But before the thing can be handed over for real money to a civil operator, there is a well established sequence of testing, checking and bargaining, and the rules are the same for everyone.

'Don't get us wrong,' said Bates anxiously. 'We're not going to cut corners in testing. What Ray means is that we started out by building four Presidents, to fly in quick succession and get stuck into the development programme.'

'In quick succession?' The warning bells started to ring. 'How quick?'

'Number two is on engine runs,' said Bates with something less than enthusiasm. 'She could fly within the next two weeks.'

# ◢6◣

Jack Old was the least enthusiastic man I had met so far. He had a good reason, for he was chief flight test engineer. The President had crashed at the end of his flight test schedule. Not only that, he was responsible for recovering the wreckage and finding out why. I was shortly to discover that these were not his only problems.

We leaned on a balcony inside a building on the northern edge of South Field, gazing at the floor below. It was a sight to leave one with a sense of unreality. The building was Number Five in Morlands' parlance. It was their highest security area. Lockheed in America had a similar setup —the 'skunk works' to their employees—where they had built the U2 and the F12. I was sure the Morlands people didn't call this building anything but Number Five, with capital-letter respect.

From my elevated position, I could see four Presidents. One was surrounded by a mass of electrical check-out gear; say a month before it would be rolled out. Another lacked one engine and various panels and windows, and would take longer. Yet another looked complete and ready to go at any time.

The fourth was taking grotesque shape immediately below us. The fin and rear twenty feet of fuselage was almost intact, the way it so often is, which is why I sit as far back as I can in any airliner. The outer wings were there too, and the twin buckled masses of the engines. In between there was a pile of blackened metal, and then some cleaner pieces nearest to me where the nose had gone so deep that the fire hadn't reached it.

No wonder Old's forty-year head had a sixty-year face.

'Where have we got to?' I asked.

'Nowhere, so far.' He sounded tired. The sight of three years' work and thirty million pounds blowing a hole in the ground had done nothing for his sleep. 'It's mostly here now,' he said. 'The railway people would've had a fit if we'd done a plot.'

'Not much point.' I wanted to console him. 'Who needs a wreckage plot when the one thing everybody agrees is that there was no structural failure?'

'That's just the trouble.' He was yet another local man. 'We all saw it, yet there's nothing obvious about it, nothing that makes sense.'

'Tell me what you mean.' I was still trying to get the feel of the thing, waiting for someone to provide an unconscious clue.

'*You* know.' He blundered about for a way of describing it. 'We don't just build a plane and fly it, do we? I mean, everything was checked twenty times over. We knew exactly how it ought to have behaved. So did John Rose.'

'John?' I pounced on the name too quickly, and caught myself glancing down at the remains of the cockpit. 'What had you done to set him up?'

'Everything we could. We've a simulator linked up to an analogue computer, so that we can make it respond like any aeroplane, real or imaginary. John flew some right bastards on there, I can tell you. And the President; he flew that on the simulator, hours of it, with every sort of failure we could throw at him.'

'But in the end, he came across one you hadn't thought of.'

'Right enough, but it wasn't for want of trying. We even built the M107.'

'What's that?'

'A half-scale President, a low-speed research plane, just a single-seater. M107 officially, Secretary for short. Half a President, see?' He actually grinned. 'John flew over a hundred hours in it.'

'What you're saying is, he shouldn't have got it wrong.'

'I'm not saying that at all. You can never *eliminate* the risks, only cut them down and down. All I'm saying is, something funny happened up there, something we'd none of us allowed for. What was it? Were we standing that close that we couldn't see?'

'What have you in the way of evidence? A good deal, I would have thought.'

'Oh, aye. A whole mess of evidence. Voice tapes, telemeter traces, cine films...' His voice petered out.

'Crash recorders?'

He stayed very quiet.

'Surely to God you didn't fly it without crash recorders!'

'She carried two,' he said with an effort. 'One in the tailcone, one in the port wingtip pod.'

'Well, then. They should tell us a good deal.' The tailcone was in good shape, and the pod looked reasonably intact.

'They've gone.' Old looked slightly green.

'You mean you can't find them?'

'I mean they've gone.'

It made no sense at all. 'What kind of recorder?'

'Our own. We've an electronics division, as you know. Stand up to anything, those recorders. Fifty-channel, eject on impact or on pilot command.'

'Then they should have been close to the crater.'

'Aye, they should've been. But they weren't.'

'You mean somebody pinched them?' One doesn't ask a man in that position whether he's looked properly. It wouldn't be the first time an idle bystander had thwarted an entire investigation by making a souvenir of some vital piece of wreckage.

'That's what it looks like.'

'*Both* of them?'

'Yes.'

'How long before your first people reached the scene? Anybody beat you to it?'

'Well, somebody must have done, mustn't they?' Old was about to lose his temper. 'Look, it crashed on t'other side of the works. The emergency services are based on North Field. It took them, what? Five or six minutes to get down to the railway line.'

'And people were there already?'

'People are *always* there already. Hell, you're the crash expert, you know. I don't know how they do it.'

'No chance that John Rose jettisoned them when he realised he was in trouble? Would they be back down the flight path?'

'Not what you'd call a chance. When you see the films, you'll realise we would have seen them, had they been fired anywhere in the last three or four minutes of flight. They weren't.'

'So in five or six minutes,' I said heavily, 'with people converging on the scene, somebody made off with two crash recorders.'

'It seems so, does it not?'

I pondered. 'Anybody tried to sell them back to you?'

'No.'

'Well, I hope somebody does.'

'What d'you mean by that?' Old was too tired to think quickly.

'I mean the alternative hardly bears thinking about.'

He frowned at me, and I realised I might already have said too much. Either that, or I was losing my grip.

## ◢7◣

Two bright orange cylinders, a foot in diameter and eighteen inches long; that was all we were lacking. I glared at Simpson and Bates and Old. 'Just tell me where they might be,' I pleaded.

'We had given the matter some thought,' said George Simpson dryly. 'We've questioned everybody we *found* at the scene, but none of them saw anything, of course.' He

27

sighed at the perpetual fear of the British at the thought of bearing witness.

'Whoever it was has had twenty-four hours. They could be anywhere by now,' I complained. 'Could they be analysed except by Morlands?'

'Only with considerable difficulty,' said Old. 'It would take the devil of a time.'

'How important *are* the recorders, anyway? What other data do we have?'

'Not enough.' Old was gloomy. 'We have the films, and the telemetry, but they merely tell us what we all saw; that the President went into a vertical climb and then spun in. We know exactly *how* she crashed, but we've still not the vaguest notion *why*.'

'That's ridiculous.' I felt angry. 'How did she get so nose-up? Can't you work back to control surface movements and power settings?'

'Yes,' said Bates. 'We're running a computer programme on it now. It'll take time, but will it get us anywhere? She went nose-up because the foreplane ran away to the nose-up position, you can see that from the film. All the computers in the world won't tell us why that runaway occurred.'

'Only the wreckage can tell us that, you mean.' They were starting to depress me with their good Yorkshire sense. 'What about the airborne records?'

'We had five thousand pounds of instrumentation in the centre fuselage,' said Bates, '*and* two flight test observers.' It was a reminder that we were thinking of four deaths, not just one.

'Is there nothing left?'

'Nothing worth a damn. That's where the explosion came,' Old explained.

'Well, then. Who takes over the flight test programme?' Perhaps the back-up pilot could offer some sense.

There was a strained silence round the table.

'Arthur Morland.' It was Simpson who came out with it. They had all foretold my reaction.

'You can't be serious.'

'He's serious,' said Bates. 'Until young Arthur came along

the Morlands had done no more than run the business. Aircraft as such didn't interest them. Arthur's different; he fought his father to get in to the technical side. Sir William was against it, but Arthur talked him round.' It all sounded rather defensive. Bates was aware of the snag. 'You're slightly prejudiced,' he ventured. 'Arthur was never a service pilot, nor at ETPS, but he's well trained and keen.'

'The saints preserve me from keen test pilots.' I felt grimmer than ever. 'Keenness and care don't mix. I hope you can keep him out of the second President until we're sure what happened to the first one.' I had heard tell of Arthur Morland.

There was a pained silence. They stared at me as though I was a raving iconoclast. 'We'll try,' muttered Old.

'You'll do better than that,' I warned, 'unless you want twice the trouble you already have.'

'Press conference in ten minutes,' said Brian Bates, looking at his watch.

'Before we go in.' I stopped them in the act of rising. 'If I say anything startling during the conference, for goodness' sake back me up. I meet these boys more often than you do, and they work with their eyes as well as their ears. Whatever I come up with, try keeping a straight face.'

'What are you thinking of coming up with?' Bates sounded worried, and rightly so.

'I'm not sure.' It was the truth. I had still to convince myself of the wisdom of a slowly-forming idea. 'It all depends which way it goes.'

# ◢8◣

The main presentation hall was in keeping with the image
of the headquarters building as a whole. It was smart, but
slightly frayed round the edges if you looked carefully. It
was extremely well equipped; dais, curtains, projectors,
microphones, in fact everything needed to stage any sort of
show. As we filed in, it looked as though we would need the
microphones. The press had done Morlands proud.

We sat down behind the table on the platform. Smythe,
the Morland Public Relations Director, took the centre.
Bates was on his left, Old and I on his right. I quartered
the small sea of heads, counted one quarter and estimated
that there must be getting on for a hundred and fifty
people facing us. In the normal way, one doesn't reckon
on raising more than thirty aviation journalists in Britain.
Less than that, maybe.

The familiar faces, the ones I knew and trusted—or dis-
trusted—were all there. As for the others, they must all
have entered with press passes. Simpson and Smythe between them would have seen to that.

'Good afternoon, ladies and gentlemen.' Smythe took us
straight into the routine. I looked around for his ladies,
and found he was right; one very familiar face in the front
row, and two unknown ones right at the back.

'As you all know,' continued Smythe, 'we had the mis-
fortune to lose an aircraft yesterday. We have received a
great many inquiries about the accident, and we thought the
fairest course was to call a conference so that we could state
the company position to everyone at the same time, in the
same way.' He did his best to make it sound as though
Morlands was doing a favour being so fair about it. Actually

they were saving themselves time and trouble, and I wondered how the bigger names would react to being dragged all the way up to Barnsdale.

'For the record,' he went on, 'the aircraft we lost was a company-financed prototype.' There was a mutter among the more knowledgeable members of the audience. Company-financed prototypes—private ventures, in other words—had gone out of fashion twenty years ago. 'I am sad to say,' Smythe continued smoothly, 'that we also lost four lives, including that of our Chief Test Pilot. This is a matter of great sorrow to us, though we are naturally thankful that no member of the public was injured.' He laid slight stress on the last few words.

'I would like to make it quite clear,' he said, 'that the aircraft concerned is the subject of strict commercial security as far as we are concerned. For that reason, I cannot tell you very much about it. You are welcome at this stage to ask questions, but I beg that you be not too offended if some of them are not answered.' And with that, he introduced us.

A small man surfaced from the front row. 'You did say commercial security?' he asked.

'Exactly so.' Smythe gave him a wintry smile.

'So it was a civil aircraft?'

Smythe had no trouble fielding that one. 'I didn't say that. I implied that it was not subject to Ministry security. In other words, it was not built to a Ministry contract. It was company-financed, and we have no interest in seeing the prospective market spoilt by any premature disclosure.' Smythe was not a Morlands' director for nothing. He had established in their minds that the aircraft could have been anything.

'We've found people round about who saw it crash,' said another journalist. 'I presume you are not expecting us to withhold their descriptions of the machine?' An unpopular man, his favourite ploy was to state the obvious as though he were scoring a point.

'I wouldn't *dream* of asking you to do that.' Smythe sounded suitably patronising. 'Once the machine had flown, it was inevitable that many people would see it. The outline is no longer a secret, though you know as well as I the tendency of some eye-witnesses to embroider.' His audience tittered appreciatively.

'*My* eye-witnesses said it was noisy and dirty.' The well-known lady in the front row floated the implication sweetly across. 'Does that indicate that it was a military aircraft of some kind?'

'Leading question, ma'am.' Smythe said it half in reproach, half as a warning to Bates. 'Brian?'

'Not necessarily.' Bates sounded grim, but well capable of staying out of trouble. 'There are very good military reasons for keeping down noise and smoke, both of which make an aircraft easier to detect. The plain fact of the matter is that noise and smoke reduction are part of any development programme. If you held the first flight until you reckoned the prototype was as clean and quiet as the production standard, you might be held up months.'

'And in the meantime, the local people have to put up with it?' It would take more than that to knock her from her hobby-horse.

All three Morlands men made to answer, but it was Old who took it up, his local accent plain to hear. 'There are local reporters here, ma'am,' he said firmly. 'That question might better have come from them. We'd not like to feel we were being *used*, like, as notional cannon-fodder.' I saw several members of the audience write that down. 'You'll appreciate,' Old went on, 'that we're not exactly the prettiest or cleanest part of the country around here. Them as don't work in Morlands mostly go down the pits. They'll complain soon enough if they hear us down there.' The questioner coloured, made to speak again and thought better of it.

'The four victims,' said another, 'who were they?'

'Pilot, co-pilot, two flight test observers.' Smythe hesitated, then gave their names. 'Now then,' he said, 'you're all after a story, I appreciate that. I also know that you can find these people's next of kin and question them. There's no secret about my opinion of that approach; I think it's very, very nasty. Apart from that, it won't get you anywhere. Everyone on the project knows what it means to the company, and has been briefed not to discuss it with anyone, not even their families.' He paused.

'We can't stop you following that line of enquiry,' he went on, 'only the people concerned can do that. But please accept my assurance that they can tell you nothing. If you need background on the four victims, the firm can supply that in detail.' There was a low hum of discussion in the audience. Most of them had noted the names. I had a fair idea which ones would try the follow-up; the ones who had come to see Liz after my Boscombe crash. They had hardly helped.

'Had you any indication of trouble before the crash came?' ventured a technical-looking lad from one of the magazines.

'None,' said Old tersely. 'Everything had gone according to plan for nigh-on an hour. There was one final garbled transmission from the pilot, no more. Then the aircraft spun in off its final approach. You all know where it landed.'

'Have British Rail raised the question of compensation?' This from a man I had never seen before.

'Not yet. But doubtless they will.' Laughter. Nobody wanted to know what John had said in his last, garbled transmission.

'Are you aware'—another unknown face—'that Morlands shares have fallen today?'

'I am. It hardly comes as a great surprise.' Smythe frowned and scribbled rapidly on his pad. I read the name of a financial journal over his shoulder before he slanted it towards Bates.

'But they've fallen a good deal,' the probing voice continued. 'I don't want to labour the point, but there is speculation that the Morlands board acted unwisely in producing an aircraft—clearly, from what we have heard, an expensive aircraft—in such unwonted secrecy. It is felt that the company might sustain a considerable loss and have to face the anger of its shareholders, who must feel they were not sufficiently consulted.'

'Is that what they think, or what you think?' Smythe's anger showed for one acid moment. 'This is pure speculation,' he said to the assembly at large. 'One has to balance

33

the confidence of well-informed shareholders against the potential profit of being alone in an untapped market. Without secrecy, we would certainly not be alone. It is,' he said in tones which spoke of conclusion, 'a very complicated point to argue here.' Perhaps, but my idea had been given a certain impetus.

'Are you confident that the cause of this crash can be quickly established?' A national daily steered us back on to course.

'Yes,' said Bates baldly.

'Have you recovered the crash recorders?'

There was a slender silence, just wide enough for me to jump in. Old might be on the verge of saying they were lost, and suddenly I wanted to stop him doing that. 'You blokes have got crash recorders on the brain,' I said. They gazed at me with interest. 'Here we have an aircraft which crashed in full view of a top-class technical team. There are cine-theodolite films, a telemetered history of the whole flight, the wreckage is being reassembled at this moment, and you ask about crash recorders!'

'But it did carry recorders?'

'Of course it did. What I'm saying is that it would be a remarkable recorder which would of itself give us the answer. A recorder tells you exactly what the aircraft *did*. The actual failure is still a matter of deduction. In this case we can *look* at what the aircraft did, over and over again, thanks to the films. The answer lies in the wreckage.'

'Did Morlands feel that AIB assistance was necessary?' A low, fast ball from one of the prestige weeklies. I was so relieved at having choked them off crash recorders that I could only look blank. Smythe rescued me.

'Technically, AIB assistance is valuable but not a necessity,' he explained. 'We thought it better to call in official representation because of other questions which might arise from the accident.'

'Such as what?' Smythe had talked his way into that one.

'The question of compensation, for one thing. It is clearly better to have a neutral observer on hand. We feel the Ministry are happier that way, for they are bound to receive representations from certain quarters. This way, they

34

are in a position to deal with them properly'. He was smoothing over my anomalous situation rather well.

'But they can't do that without knowing about the aircraft.'

'Up to a point, that is so.' I don't know why Smythe chose to put it that way, but I felt the eyes swivelling towards me.

'Mr Goddard.' A grating voice from the second row. 'Are you receiving full co-operation from Morlands?'

'Absolutely.'

'Your function is not one of sitting waiting for the firm's answer?'

'By no means.' It was up to me to slap him down. 'I am taking an active part in the whole investigation. I am, after all, an engineer, and I was a test pilot.'

'And how much do *you* know about this secret aeroplane?'

'Technically, everything,' I said grimly. 'But I'm obliged to regard what I know as confidential. I'll not tell you anything Morlands won't. You'll gain nothing by cross-examining me.' I grinned to take some of the sting out of it.

'Do you share Mr Bates' confidence that the cause of the crash will be quickly found?'

'Yes, I do.' He had given me the opening I needed. 'I have already explained how well placed we are to analyse the behaviour of the aircraft up to the point where control was lost. The number of possible causes is limited, and the wreckage will give us the answer.'

'You think it was a failure of some kind?'

'The only alternative is pilot error. For more than one reason, I don't believe that.'

'There is always, surely, the possibility of a design fault.' This was an American voice from somewhere in the middle of the floor. It shook me that they should have thought it worthwhile to send somebody, let alone do it so quickly.

'In this day and age, the possibility of a design fault is almost non-existent. What with computers, wind tunnels, rig tests and accumulated experience, very little can go wrong.'

'That's what we were saying, until the F14.' The American F14 had crashed on its second flight, because vibration had fractured an unsupported hydraulic pipe.

'I don't believe this aircraft faced that sort of problem.'

They waited for me to say something else, but I couldn't do it without giving away a little of the President's make-up.

'What about sabotage?'

'Sabotage.' I tried to give the impression I was chewing it over. 'It's the first thing everybody thinks of, and it almost never happens. It makes a lovely story for you boys, but you must beware of jumping to conclusions. Look at the Comet disasters; all the circumstances pointed to sabotage, but it was nothing of the kind.'

'No,' said the American voice. 'It was a design fault.'

'We were thinking about sabotage.' I chopped him off before his sense of comedy ran away with him. 'With sabotage, you have to start work on detective lines: motive and opportunity.' They waited with quiet expectation. 'In this case the motive can only be vague and the opportunity was non-existent, because of the security screen behind which the aircraft was built. I'm afraid sabotage is a red herring.'

I wanted to leave it at that, lest they thought I protested too much, but Smythe misread the situation and destroyed my opening. 'Somebody mentioned the local press a while back,' he said, seeking to change the course of events. 'Have they no questions?'

'The local press is still rather stunned.' The acoustics of the hall were good, but the quality of the voice surprised me. It was one of the girls at the back, speaking with just a hint of local accent. 'I imagine there are two things we should know,' she went on. 'How will it affect employment at Morlands, and what happens if the next one comes down more to the west, in the town? You see,' she said apologetically, 'I saw it happen. It turned over Barnsdale, did it not, and it might have come down there as well as anywhere.'

Smythe coughed, embarrassed, thinking up his quick answer. 'First,' he smiled down the hall, 'the programme will not be seriously delayed by what has happened.

There is no question of redundancy, least of all in the proto-type shops where the second aircraft is now—er, taking shape. Beyond that, there should be a production run sufficient to keep us looking for workers through the 1970s.' He enjoyed that. 'As to your *other* point,' he said, and clearly he had been thinking fast, 'we believe that this was a very isolated incident. Morlands has been building aircraft here since before the first war, and the last one to crash in the local area did so in 1917.'

'Could I make a point?' I butted in before he could get going again. 'We are almost sure the aircraft had to crash where it did, on short finals. The town was never in any danger.' There was another buzz in the audience, and I saw that Bates had forgotten my advice about keeping a straight face. I hoped nobody would attach too much significance to the fact that he looked as though he had never heard such nonsense in his life.

He was in good company; neither had I.

'What on earth was the idea of that?' he demanded after I had rebutted the inevitable aftermath and played hard to get until the journalists had retired in frustration. Now I had Bates and Old and Simpson to deal with. For all my reservations, my approach to them had to be different.

'You're not going to like this,' I warned.

'Going to?' Brian Bates snorted. 'I don't like it now. If I was hearing straight, you said the President had to crash where it did. Fair enough; tell me what you know and I so obviously don't.'

'You know everything I know, Brian. It's simply that you're unwilling to draw the inevitable conclusion.'

'Which is?'

'Look at it this way. What are the possible causes of this crash? Technical failure, pilot error—and sabotage.'

'You were at great pains to rule out sabotage during the press conference,' Simpson pointed out.

'Of course I was. I'm not completely irresponsible.'

'You've still to convince me of that,' said Bates.

'None of the journalists know what we know—that the crash recorders have gone missing. That was why I deliber-

37

ately played down their importance. But they *have* gone missing, and what conclusion can we come to?'

'Somebody picked them up.' Simpson looked at me thoughtfully.

'Not only did he pick them up, he knew what he was looking for. Worse still, he was waiting for them to arrive.'

There was a glum silence in the little room.

'You see now, don't you? In less than five minutes, somebody picked up both recorders—and they may well have been a few hundred yards apart—and made off with them. That couldn't have been done without prior knowledge of where the President would crash. Accept that, and you accept sabotage, agreed?'

'You realise,' said Simpson quietly, 'that you imply I have fallen down on my job?'

'That's a harsh self-judgement, George. It couldn't have been done without knowing a great deal about the aircraft. In other words, it must have been partly an inside job. Of course, you could always have done it yourself.'

'I suppose so.' His smile was slightly bleak. 'You mean we can't trust anybody.'

'I thought very hard before telling you three. We certainly shouldn't tell more people than really need to know.' I was interested that they appeared to accept the theory without reservation, perhaps because it let them off the hook to some extent. Except George Simpson, of course.

'He was a bit of a mug to pick up the recorders, wasn't he?' said Jack Old.

'Presumably he felt that was less of a risk than leaving them to be found. He could always count on the natural reluctance to accept sabotage as an explanation.'

'But why would anyone want to do it?'

'Grudge,' said Simpson tersely. 'Gain,' he went on. 'Nutcase,' he concluded.

'Well organised, for a nutcase,' said Old.

'Grudge or gain, then. Plenty of people with a grudge, and who knows who might gain?'

'That, at least,' I said, 'is something we might look into.'

Rather than commit me to the middle of Barnsdale, Morlands had booked me into the Anglers Arms, which squatted in grey-stoned obstinacy in one of the small villages to the south. Fortunately, it was better inside than it looked from the car park. It was late when the company car set me down outside; the gloom was gathering, the October wind hurried across the moor, and brought with it the threat of rain. I needed an evening to myself, to drink and brood.

In that, I was unlucky. Whoever had booked me the room, it couldn't have been Simpson, he would have known better. I had hardly set foot inside the bar when the cry went up.

'Look out, folks, it's the Government Inspector.' Armstrong was well into his third pint and laying down the law to his fellow journalists, yet not so engrossed as to fail to spot me straight away. I cursed, and hardly under my breath. 'Neil!' he ploughed on, 'are you sharing our humble abode?'

'It looks like it, doesn't it?' It was too late to retreat.

'Come and have one with us. Off the record.' He winked. The others manoeuvred to leave an inviting gap in the circle. It was a long time since I had been so popular.

'Off the record, a pint. And nothing else.'

'Oh, come *on*.' Familiarity bred easy contempt in Armstrong. 'All that business about knowing why it happened.' He had been covering crashes since before I started having them.

'I didn't say that. You should know better than to quote people out of context.'

'Don't be like that, old boy. How else would most of us make a living?' His smile took on a more determined set as he passed across my pint.

'In that case, I'd better not say anything, had I?'

'Conspiracy of silence. Does Government share air firm's guilty secret?' The ready-made headline was thrown down by a familiar-sounding voice from the corner. I was able to put a face to the American for the first time. He caught my eye and grinned.

'Harvey MacPherson, Mr Goddard.' He leaned forward and stretched out a long arm. 'Glad to know you.' His

39

other arm was half way round a girl. She put her head on one side and looked at me as though I were a museum exhibit. I was less than happy about MacPherson; delete the 'guilty' from his quote, I thought, and you would be somewhere near the truth.

'I imagined,' I said to the company at large, 'that you'd be flogging down the motorway by now, to file your stories.' It was more of a pious hope, but what were they all doing here?

'They're filed,' chuckled Armstrong. 'God bless the telephone.'

'And what has Yorkshire got that London can't offer?' He was beginning to annoy me.

'Story, old boy.' He tapped the side of his nose and conjured up a barman with a magic wave of his other hand over his empty glass. 'What are Morlands up to?'

'Building aeroplanes, like always.' I sensed something interesting in the line he was taking.

'But what sort of aeroplane?' asked MacPherson. 'And why keep it so dark?' His hold on the girl was better established.

This had to stop. I hadn't the patience to draw it out of them by degrees. 'Davie,' I said to Armstrong, 'how well do you know me?'

'Oh boy,' he giggled, 'do I know you.'

'Then you know it's a waste of time probing around. You'll get nothing out of me bar what I want to tell you, and I'll give you that for free.' They stayed respectfully silent while I drank, waiting for what I wanted to tell them.

'Tell me something for a change,' I said, and they groaned in unison. 'No, look; what are you all doing here? There were faces at that conference I'd never seen before. Financial people, industrial correspondents, so Smythe says. And MacPherson, here; he's not London-based. Come all the way from New York, did you?'

'Washington.'

'There you are. Dozens of you, like vultures round a carcass. Not only do you appear, you stay. What's the whisper? Why the interest?'

'There's the coroner's court the day after tomorrow.'

'And the rest,' I retorted. 'The coroner's not going to hear any more than you have. Evidence of identification, strenuous efforts are being made and thank you all very much, adjourned for a month. Your editors would have your hides if you were taking two days out of the office to hear *that*.'

'As you say.' A sharper voice came from beside me, a small, smart man to contrast with Armstrong's untidy bulk. I didn't know him. 'The street seems to think there's a big, complicated story here somewhere.'

'Why would they think that?'

'Somebody must have dropped a hint. There are the share prices, you know; Morlands dipped badly today. It could be a case of putting two and two together, but the impression is that somebody really knows something.'

'I see.' This was more the sort of thing. 'The money boys are playing fast and loose in London, are they? Anybody interested in who, exactly?'

'If it's anything like that,' said the finance man, quick to catch my drift, 'they'll have covered their tracks carefully.'

'Goddard's better placed than us to find out,' Armstrong said amiably, 'with his contacts.'

'What *are* his contacts?'

I almost jumped. It was MacPherson's girl who had spoken, and I recognised in her the cool, clear voice from the back of the hall; the local reporter who had seen it happen.

'He married them, ducky.' Armstrong had covered my Boscombe crash, and turned up at most of my investigating jobs. A technical nonentity, his strength was background stuff. 'Marry money,' he went on, 'marry power, marry contacts. His father-in-law was tax-dodging consultant to the best of them.'

The girl looked at me with something like sympathy. 'Poor Mr Goddard. A foot in both camps, is that it?'

'Something like that. The trick is to stop them moving too far apart.' Armstrong spluttered mirth.

'I don't get it,' I said innocently. 'It's possible that somebody is looking for a financial angle—a way to make money in a falling market—but technically the story is simple enough. It will all be there in the tapes and the wreckage. We'll have it cleared up inside the week.'

'Mr Goddard,' murmured MacPherson, 'I think you just got yourself back on the record.'

Maybe, but nobody had even mentioned crash recorders. That at least was a relief.

# ◢9◣

If it *was* in the wreckage, we couldn't find it. There was nothing to account for the way the President had suddenly gone out of control. True, the nose section was in poor shape but by the end of the next day we had traced the whole run of the elevator circuit and there was nothing wrong with it. It wasn't much of a run, just a few feet of push-pull rod to the foreplane power control units in the cabin roof aft of the cockpit, and most of it had avoided any fire damage. The control units themselves were in fair shape. We took them out, cleaned them up and rig-tested them, and they behaved exactly as they should have done.

The computers were going full bore on the problem from their end, but nobody was confident they would give us an answer. People were doing their best to salvage the taped data from the ravaged main instrument banks. There was still no sign of the crash recorders. Search teams had combed the crash area yet again without success, and George Simpson's local information network was on the alert, all to no avail. It had been agreed that we dared not make the loss public.

In the afternoon, in a state of growing desperation, I

asked if I could fly the M107, the half-scale President test vehicle. Old looked startled at first but he had no very good reason for stopping me. By another of those legal quirks, all a test pilot needs is an ordinary private pilot's licence. I had both that, and the background to cope. Eventually he arranged to have the aircraft cleared for flight the next afternoon. It was about that time that Morland's secretary came through, asking me to dine with the Chairman that evening.

To my surprise, Sir William Morland looked slightly the worse for drink, or maybe it was me. He glared at me over the brandy.

'They tell me you think it was sabotage.' It was the first thing he had said about the President all evening. We had no audience save the brooding presence of Sir James Lovegrove, the firm's resident financial genius. Sir James frowned at the mention of so unsavoury a word.

'Sabotage,' said Morland, rubbing it in; 'I thought you people never believed in sabotage.'

'We believe in anything that fits the facts.' I looked from one to the other. 'I've spent most of today digging out facts that contradict any other explanation.' They were both glaring at me. 'There is no sign of any technical failure in the ordinary sense,' I went on, 'and nobody really believes in pilot error as an explanation.'

'Maybe not,' said Morland. 'But sabotage is only an artificially induced technical failure, surely. How can you say there was no failure, yet believe in sabotage?'

He was right, of course. 'Sabotage covers a wider field than straightforward wrecking,' I protested. 'There's nothing obviously wrong, so we're up against a subtle saboteur. Anyway, the loss of the crash recorders suggests I'm right. The President was got at. Who would have wanted to get at it?'

Morland grunted, glanced across at Lovegrove. 'All sorts of people.' It sounded as though he wanted to leave it at that.

'If President went bad on you,' I ventured, 'could you survive?'

There was a sharp intake of breath from Lovegrove. 'Really, Goddard.' He sounded like a reproving school-master. 'You have already been given more information than I would have advised. That question far exceeds anything you have a right to ask.'

'It wouldn't exactly finish us,' said Morland suddenly. Lovegrove looked at him, appalled. 'By heck,' the old man went on, 'it would give us a nasty time for a month or so. It might finish us for aircraft, you can see that.'

'Really, William.' Lovegrove was outraged. 'I take no responsibility for admitting that outside the boardroom.'

'Stop snivelling, James.' The juggernaut Morland had decided on the course to be taken. 'Mr Goddard's position is privileged already,' he snapped. 'Mr Goddard is an un-usual man. His father-in-law would probably have swung the whole thing on the treasury for us.'

'Father-in-law?'

'Andrew Wallace.'

'Oh.' A whole series of expressions chased across Love-grove's face.

'Why would it only finish you for aircraft?' I prompted.

'Think, lad. We're diverse enough—electronics, materials, property; we'd survive. But if we dropped thirty million on a project that went wrong, we'd have to capitalise. And nobody would underwrite an aircraft division after a débâcle like that.' This time, Lovegrove said not a word. His face was back under control.

'Who wants you out of the aircraft business?' I could have sworn Lovegrove relaxed slightly.

A smaller man might have jibbed at the direct question, but once committed, Morland didn't turn a hair. 'Take your choice. The Ministry, for one.'

'My Ministry,' I reminded him.

'Your Ministry.' He wouldn't flinch. 'They've been on at us for years to merge with this group or that, co-operate with the French or the Germans, all the usual things. Sheer political expediency at best, dogma at worst.'

'I rather gathered you were on speaking terms with the Minister.'

'Barry Mayhew? He's all right. But what's a minister?

44

A minister is not a Ministry,' he pontificated. 'A Ministry is a collection of civil servants, mostly permanent.'

'But the Ministry would never get mixed up in sabotage?' I hadn't meant it to sound like a question.

Morland just stared at me. 'It's a bitter business, lad,' he said at last. 'We've been involved in a polite war with them longer than most. We've lost contracts by not toeing the line. Do I have to tell you? "What a very good aeroplane, Sir William. Just the sort of thing you should be building as a joint venture with Westward. I'm sure a large contract would be forthcoming on those lines." So you tell them to get stuffed and they go and buy a second-rate design from somebody who'll do as he's told. When more and more of our sales went overseas, they started finding reasons why we shouldn't sell. Half the bloody world is embargoed as far as we're concerned. Yet still we're making money; there's those who find that hard to stomach. It proves they were wrong, you see, and it just won't do.'

'Who else?' He had given me only half an answer.

'All sorts of people. Not aircraft people, necessarily, however much you wonder. Our engineers and technicians and facilities are coveted by all manner of industry. And then,' he added heavily, 'you've the do-gooders. Ten years ago we didn't have a complaint about noise. Now we have dozens, daily. There's those that would like to see us go—neighbours who won't speak to me; they'd rather see our shop-floor men down the mine than have an aircraft fly over their precious gardens.'

'What you're saying,' I countered, 'is that the list is almost endless, and most of it would normally be regarded as above suspicion.'

'History, Mr Goddard.' For a moment I wondered what he was talking about. 'You'll understand nothing without history,' he went on. 'My father wasn't a pioneer of aviation, a Handley Page or a de Havilland or a Roe; he was a Yorkshireman who'd made his brass in wool and steel, and had the sense to back a few bright lads in the early days. They built the planes; he provided the capital and the business skill. It was he that built the firm, step by step. He

45

was always one jump ahead in the principle of the thing.'
I waited to see what was coming.

'He bought land, Goddard. He saw that to stay one of
the biggest firms in the industry, Morlands needed room
to expand. Result; we had the first hard runway in the
country. The first six thousand foot runway on an industry
airfield. It's still the best industry airfield by a long way.
All coal beneath; like I said, those that don't work for us
go down t'mine.' He gulped his brandy.

'It went further than that. In the thirties, Morlands
staked their all on a military aircraft programme. They
were calling us warmongers until 1938. It paid off, we made
a lot of money out of the war, I'll not deny that; because
we were ready. Then, in forty-three, half the design office
was working on civil projects. If they'd known at the time,
they'd have had our guts for that. But by heaven, weren't
they glad to have the results after the war! And we made
more money, and more enemies. Do you see now? It's
been going on for years. Most of my lifetime, you might
say.'

'I see.' It was easy to build up a picture of the bitterness
and frustration outside. 'They can't break you altogether,
but they can push you out of aircraft.' I paused for effect.
'Or, of course, they could just be out to make a lot of
money.'

'What do you mean?' Lovegrove was on to it like a flash.
I had almost forgotten him. His animation startled me; I
had done no more than follow the line fed me by the
financial journalists.

'Well,' I said, 'what we have here is a classic selling short
situation, isn't it? Anybody who contracted to sell Morland
shares should be able to buy in for half price before settlement day.' Surely he didn't need that spelling out to him,
not the financial wizard?

'Disgusting.' He meant it. 'We are talking of four lives
lost. Who would do that for profit?' He had gone very
pale.

'But the shares *are* well down. I wonder if anyone contracted to sell recently? Can you find out?'

'I can find out if it was done, not necessarily who has

done it. I need hardly tell you about nominees.' Lovegrove hesitated. 'William,' he said to Morland, 'shall we do that?'

'Yes. Let's have it out in the open. You never know.'

'Very well.' Lovegrove looked pained in the extreme. He was about to say something when the door opened. The newcomer was tall, slender, fair-haired; pushing thirty, but not very hard. His step had a bounce and his eyes a sparkle.

'Arthur,' said Morland, confirming that I was about to meet the new Chief Test Pilot.

'I've heard of you,' said Arthur Morland as we were introduced. 'You've been hard at work already, I hear. Do you think you will ever find out what John did wrong?'

I tried to size him up, this young man who had fought his father and won. Was it a stubborn streak, or was every aspect of his character as strong? 'The only thing John did wrong,' I said grimly, 'was fly the aircraft.'

'Come now.' He smiled charmingly. 'There's nothing wrong with the aircraft.'

'There was nothing wrong with the pilot.' He must have sensed my antagonism, because he stepped back a pace and laughed again, less easily, shrugging it off. It suddenly occurred to me that I would rather Arthur wasn't told of the sabotage theory.

'We've had sabotage mentioned as a genuine possibility.' Lovegrove's thin voice caught me unawares. Arthur's smile widened.

'Sabotage! What has George Simpson been doing all this time, if not putting the tightest possible net round the whole thing? I know Mr Goddard doesn't want to see John take the blame without good reason, but where else is there a weak link? What about heart failure? Did John Rose simply pass out amid the tension of the final approach?' He paused to add weight to his argument.

'Now look,' he said, turning to face me once more. 'There's nothing wrong with the President. When number two is ready to go, she goes. That's my job, now.'

# ◢10◣

I'll say one thing for Arthur Morland, he might almost
have had the coroner's ear. It went mostly as we had expected, except for the medical evidence. The coroner was
an elderly man, not to be hurried, determined to be thor-
ough in front of the biggest audience of his career. He
took evidence of identification and then hauled in the
pathologist.

'We have heard,' he said in measured tones, 'that identification was of necessity a rather *formal* procedure.' What
he meant was that none of the bodies had been even remotely recognisable. 'Have you tried to obtain by post-
mortem examination whether any of the crew were incapacitated *before* impact?' He might have been asking
whether a dead driver had been drinking.

'I can certainly say that the two passengers from the
main body of the aircraft were not so incapacitated. Death
in their case was immediate upon impact.'

'Quite so. And the pilots?'

'Nobody could say with certainty. The state of the
bodies was not compatible with a full autopsy. There was
no positive result from any test for alcohol or drugs, but
that is about as far as I can go.'

'So it is possible,' said the dreadful old man, 'that the
pilot might have suffered a cardiac or cerebral failure?'

'It is possible, certainly. I can do nothing to confirm it.'

'Or eliminate the possibility.' The coroner nodded.

The evidence of Morlands' own medical superintendent
was that neither pilot had any history of trouble and both
had been in excellent health at the time of their last checks.

'There was no special check before this flight?'

'No, sir.'

'I see.' There was something about the way he said it.

Then it was my turn.

'So far,' he leered at me, 'you have discovered nothing that might have caused this aircraft to crash?'

'Not yet. But the investigation is at a very early stage. We have a great deal of data to sift, not to mention the wreckage itself.'

'I see. And are your investigations aimed at finding a fault in the aircraft, or in its crew?'

'Our investigations,' I said warningly, 'are aimed at finding out what happened. We will neither discard nor accept any explanation unless we are fully satisfied.'

'Quite.' He coughed, and looked around the room to see who was writing it all down. 'I would certainly hope that, in the absence of any mechanical explanation, you will not forget the medical possibilities.'

'I have already said we will not.' The old devil was determined to get it across.

'Are there any more Ministry witnesses?'

I wasn't sure whether he was asking me or the Clerk.

'No, sir.'

'You are the *only* Ministry representative taking part in the investigation?'

'Yes.'

'Is that entirely *wise*?' He frowned and leaned forward, but failed to look any wiser himself.

'My function is partly that of observer.' The need to pick my words with care built up the tension within. 'The manufacturers are absolutely competent to carry out the full investigation. I hold a watching brief for the Ministry and I am, naturally, fully qualified to assist technically.'

'And has such assistance been sought?' He blinked at me owlishly. 'Do you, for instance, have access to the crash recorders?'

The suddenness of it took me by surprise. I fumbled for a moment, then said, 'I have as much access to the recorder traces as any member of Morlands' technical staff.' In absolute terms, that was perfectly true, however misleading.

'You are satisfied that you are being kept sufficiently well informed?'

'Yes, certainly.'

'I am glad to hear it. I feel that for the moment, you are in a more fortunate position than this court.' It wasn't a question, so I didn't provide an answer. The tension built up once more. There was a stir somewhere behind me, a rustle of paper as a shorthand notebook was turned over expectantly. The coroner glared at me, then transferred his attention to his Clerk.

'Any more witnesses?'

# ◢11◣

I had been away from serious flying too long. The half-scale President was beautifully built and a fine advertisement for Morlands, but it wasn't a quick aeroplane. It had plenty of power for the take-off and climb and it was a minute or two before I caught up mentally. After that, I started to enjoy it; the feel of mask and helmet and suit, all the things I had missed in the Piper. I spent twenty minutes getting the feel of the thing, looking for the unexpected and failing to find it. Bates and his team had done a good job, even on this little flying laboratory which was meant strictly for expert hands.

Eventually I had to get down to work, which was to fly the approach, looking for snags. I turned finals over the grimy, sprawling mass of Barnsdale and straightened out, checking the landmarks, looking for the big runway in the grim visibility. The speed came back and I switched on the flap blowing, feeling the extra lift as the high-pressure air swept across the surfaces.

Nothing felt even remotely wrong. There was a gentle nose-up trim change as the flap blowing took effect; it increased slowly as the speed fell away. I held it with ease. She still rolled crisply to left and right as I waggled the stick. The view on the approach was fantastic, the best I had ever encountered. Gradually, the runway took shape. I had a vague feeling that something was wrong, then realised what it was; the crater had gone. Where two days ago there had been a big hole in the ground and lots of severed railway line, now there was no more than a scar of fresh earth. The trains were back on their normal route to London.

We settled on to the runway, the aircraft and I, and the ground effect cushioned us. I hardly had to ease back on the stick at all and we greased on, keeping straight with ease. Then I switched off the blowing and went round again.

It was depressing. Two more circuits failed to suggest even remotely what might have happened to the President. I tried overshooting from various stages of the approach, in case John really *had* baulked at the landing and uncovered some hidden effect when he had opened the throttles. Still there was nothing. The M107 was as viceless and easy to fly as any basic trainer. After an hour of it I landed, tired as much by the disappointment as by the concentration.

They had given me an office in Number Five building, close to the President assembly hall. It was a long drive back from the main flight-test sheds, but Old gave me a lift, enthusing the while about my flying. I had been good, once; it was nice to find somebody who thought I still was. Liz, you bitch.

The October evening gathered fast, and the lights were on. I wandered through the building, nodding to the faces which were becoming familiar. What a place, what a hive of activity! It was as though they were leaving the day before yesterday and the big hole in the moor to me, while they built for the morrow.

It lay on my desk—my otherwise forlorn, empty desk; one of those big brown envelopes, its face split into rectangles for a succession of addressees, which carries internal mail in any firm with more than a hundred employees. I opened it without interest. The note was typewritten and brief.

'Who was selling shares? And who is *checking* who sold shares?'

That was all. It was a clear enough pointer to Lovegrove, and it raised two questions. Was it serious? And whether it was or not, who hated Lovegrove enough to do it? It could have been a genuine hint, a piece of petty spite, or a deliberate red herring. The envelope was a fresh one, there was no previous recipient's name to follow up. As for the typing, a big enough search would uncover the machine, but why bother? Apart from the chaos it would cause, Morlands had hundreds of typewriters, all accessible to hundreds of people. There was no mistake in the typing, which meant it was the work of an expert—or of a novice being very careful. If one accepted the possibility of a double bluff, and I did, the note provided no clue at all.

One thing was certain. There would be no harm in taking it at face value and checking up on Lovegrove. I needn't even put anybody on to checking the share register, simply as if Lovegrove had been checking. I reached for the internal phone.

Not many people had direct access to Morland, but I had insisted on it. He was sharp and to the point. 'I told him to check, didn't I? Yes, I confirmed by memo this morning.'

It was as I thought, business was business for Morland even when conducted over brandy at midnight. I reached for the outside line, then thought better of it. One never knew who might be listening. Instead, I called for a car to take me to the Anglers Arms.

Some of them had gone home after the inquest, it seemed, but not all. Armstrong was still testing the bar counter for strength and the cellar for capacity. Lacking an audience of the size to which he was accustomed, he had quietened down a good deal and contented himself with muttering to Harvey MacPherson. I slipped past the bar door unscathed. There was no sign of MacPherson's girl, the young local reporter.

It didn't take long to locate the people I wanted. By tomorrow I would know whether Lovegrove had been checking as instructed. After that, I settled down to the less pleasant task of trying to reach Liz. The longer I left it, the worse it would be. It strained my credulity to find her at home, but she wasted no time telling me that was where I belonged, too.

'The Anglers Arms?' She had one of those unmistakable voices, the kind that emerge unscathed from a long-distance line, clear and neutral. 'My darling, how rustic!'

'It's not rustic, it's Yorkshire. The wind howls over the moors and batters at the solid stone walls, and they serve nowt but tripe and onions in the dining room.'

'Are you sober?'

Bitch; when did you last laugh at anything I said, unless I was trying to be serious? 'Yes. Stone cold sober. I've only just arrived back from the works.'

'Have they given you a nice aeroplane to play with?'

'It'll do.'

'And how long do you intend staying up there? God, Neil, everyone's asking me where you are. How can I tell them you're in Barnsdale of all places? You should see them *look*.'

'I'm surprised half of them have even heard of it. You should come up here, Liz, it would do you good. They either dig coal or build aeroplanes. Real people, earning an honest living.'

'Darling, they wouldn't be happy doing anything else. Why don't you leave them to it? I'm fed up with you try-ing to close ranks with the salt of the earth.' She made them sound lower than the low. 'Come back and have some *fun*, darling. You're such a drear when you get engrossed. I'm lonely, Neil.' The change of mood was too sudden to be convincing. 'I miss you.'

'Then bring your black up here, and I'll take you to John's funeral.'

'You've made it a personal thing because of that, haven't you? Neil, love, if I'd let you go on flying, they might be burying you.'

'Liz, I'm staying up here until I find out what killed John. I don't care how long it takes. If you don't like the idea, tough; you can go and take a running jump.'

53

'Oh God, you're going native.' Her laugh was an ugly thing, tinged with scorn.

'It depends where you're standing.' I hung up, shaking, before I could launch myself into some of the choicer dialect phrases. Then I went down to wash it out of my system.

'It's beyond me.' Bert Partington was superintendent of Number Five, which gave him responsibility beyond that of many white-collar men on the other side of the airfield. 'Disturbed, you see, but nothing taken.'

'That might have been difficult.'

'But look what the chap did anyway! What's a little risk on top of so big a one?'

We were looking at the wreckage of the President. During the last three days it had been better and better sorted, even arranged on frames so that no piece could conceal another. And some of the pieces had been disturbed.

'Noticed as soon as we came in,' said Bert. 'It's one of the special areas, see? Elevator control circuit. Frames one-seventy to two-twenty-three. But nothing's gone, it's just been mucked about.'

Whoever had mucked it about was well away. According to the book on the Number Five gate, one of Bert's foremen had been last out, an hour after the end of the evening shift. We had just found the real foreman in one of the toilets, and he hadn't come round yet.

'Let's get this straight,' I said to Simpson. 'Somebody came into Number Five yesterday—difficult, not impossible. Even your blokes are human. He must have hung around unquestioned for a long time, which means he knew the ropes and looked as though he belonged. Then he knocks off the foreman, waits until everybody bar the security people are out, does his probe of the wreckage as calm as you like and finally walks out on the foreman's pass.'

'Yes,' said George. 'I'd just about worked that out for myself, thanks.'

'Yes, but it's what I *can't* work out that has me worried. Why take the risk? He didn't want to take anything with him, or he'd have taken it. So why not just mingle, have his look and then slide out?'

'He couldn't just have mingled, Mr Goddard.' Bert shook his head. 'We've only thirty blokes sorting the wreck, see, and they're almost a family, like. Had anyone else come close, they'd have wanted to know why. And if he wasn't cleared for Number Five, he'd have been in real trouble then, wouldn't he?'

'Fair enough, Bert, so he had to wait until everybody else had gone. But what was his interest? It must have been something important, yet he took nothing, you say.'

'Not a thing. It's all there.'

'Then what on earth was he up to?'

'He didn't need to take anything,' suggested Simpson. 'He had only to make sure the evidence he was scared might exist, didn't.' George looked worried.

'It certainly makes sense that he confined his search to the elevator circuit.'

'There is that to it,' said George. 'It proves we're on the right track. Come to that,' he went on, 'it proves we've shifted them. Your press conference bombshell must have made somebody sit up.'

'That's fine, George, but I don't know how to keep them on the move. They may cover their tracks before I can dream up anything else.' I didn't tell him about the note.

According to my spies, Lovegrove had not only checked, he had tried very hard. I didn't know whether or not to feel disappointed. The airfield was clamped, gloomy under a windless industrial pall. I grew steadily more miserable. Who had tried to put the finger on Lovegrove? Why the red herring? Or had I not been subtle enough?

President 02 was almost ready to fly. Whatever had happened to 01, we surely couldn't be in for a repeat performance. Everyone was on his guard now—except Arthur Morland, who would be sitting in the left hand seat.

It was about my lowest point in the whole affair. I forced myself back to first principles. *Why* had the President been sabotaged? Because Morlands was vulnerable, and the President programme was a perfect target. Of course, nobody outside Morlands was supposed to know of its existence. Did that make sense of the Lovegrove idea? The man knew all about the President, would have costed the pro-gramme as a whole. But did he have the contacts on the works side, the means to carry out the sabotage itself?

That brought me to my major stumbling block. I still had no idea how the trick had been worked. We had drawn an utter blank in the wreckage, and last night's visitor seemed to have satisfied himself that there was nothing to find. We might yet end up having to accept the coroner's view that John's heart had given out. That would please Arthur Morland—until the same thing happened to him. After all, if Morlands were the ultimate target, what better than to write off Arthur and the second aircraft at one fell swoop? Unless Arthur himself had got rid of John out of sheer envy.

The whole thing was a nightmare. The more one thought, the more possibilities there seemed to be. At least there was no doubt now that it *was* sabotage, even if it could never be admitted. The disturbance of the wreckage, added to the disappearance of the crash recorders, made that certain in my mind.

Whatever form the sabotage had taken, the man behind it must be high in technical ability, and familiar with the aircraft. In other words, he was somewhere close to me at this moment. Close enough to leave a cryptic message about Lovegrove? But in that case, he would have been close enough to check the wreckage without taking the risk some-body had accepted.

Again, who had removed the crash recorders? Clearly not the man in Morlands. The thing must have been a team effort. I recalled Simpson pinning down the motive to gain or grudge. But a grudge man would have worked alone; therefore we were left with some form of gain. Love-grove came back into sharp focus.

I was an idiot. Of course Lovegrove had checked, because he knew I could—would—check on him. I remembered the blandness slipping from his face in the second when he was told who I was. I lifted the phone, and put through the call.

'Not *again*.' I had been waking up better since coming

56

to Morlands, but not so well as to take in Simpson's greeting the next morning.

'Again.' His voice avoided any hint of expression. 'This time, a nice determined break-in.'

'Tell me some more.' He couldn't have been liking it, Number Five building was almost the centre of his security system, and it had been pierced two nights running.

'They came up the mineral railway that divides North and South Fields. The wire at the back of the building was cut, the alarms short-circuited.'

'And the wreckage?'

'Same again. Fiddled with, but at first glance nothing taken. Partington and his boys are still checking.'

'George,' I said, 'he's all right, is he, Bert Partington? I mean, he's close enough to know what's going on. A man like that can put two and two together.'

'Don't worry about Bert. He knows what'll happen if the news gets around.' His internal phone rang.

'Well, now.' He put it down after listening for no more than ten seconds, and looked almost pleased. 'Once again, our visitors left empty-handed. Nothing is missing at all.'

'So they still haven't found what they were looking for. What is it that worries them so much?'

'You tell me,' said Simpson. 'They'll not get a third chance, you can depend on that.'

It was falling into place. About the middle of the morning I finally heard about Lovegrove. It would cost me something when I returned to London, but it was worth a good deal.

There *had* been some forward selling of Morlands shares; no single big deal, but it added up to something substantial. In the normal way there would have been nothing to point to Lovegrove, no traceable connection. But some of my contacts specialised in untraceable connections; they were part of my marital inheritance.

What it boiled down to was that Sir James had agreed to sell Morland shares at a certain price on a certain day. There is nothing wrong with that if you have the shares to sell, but he hadn't; his holding in the company was small.

57

Morland himself was the only really large block holder.

Indeed, it emerged pretty clearly that Lovegrove was far from well off, and might even be in overall debt. He had become entangled in a web of other people's money. If Morlands' shares continued their plunge, he would be able to buy as many as he needed before settlement day and take the profit when he re-sold at the agreed, pre-crash price. All very risky; or had he made sure there was no risk by crashing the President?

He had certainly not done it himself, he wasn't a technical man. His shop-floor contacts must be non-existent. He must have bought or blackmailed assistants somehow. They would have no idea who was behind the scheme, a man like Lovegrove would act through intermediaries almost from sheer force of habit. His team must be extensive, since some of it had been on hand to retrieve the crash recorders. The snag with a big team, I thought, is that it presents a larger target.

It all held together beautifully, except that I still didn't know what they had done to the President. The elevator control circuit was the key to it all, that much had been obvious even from the crash film, and they had made two attempts to retrieve the physical evidence; yet their searching had failed to find it, and presumably *they* knew what they were looking for. It was small wonder we had had no luck.

Would they try again? They must know by now that security would be stepped up, that they stood a good chance of being third time unlucky. That would make them doubly anxious, and it might be a good time to try pushing them off balance. I would have to try; if they sat tight and nothing happened, they could safely assume that any proof had been lost forever. Lovegrove might well hear of my checking his financial dealings—might even assume I knew; but a morally doubtful financial manoeuvre was a far cry from proof of sabotage. If, on the other hand, he thought we had proof . . . I called Simpson.

'George,' I said, 'can you do something for me?'

'Probably.' He still sounded embarrassed.

'Call off the special security guard on the wreckage.'

'I presume you have a reason.'

'Of course I've a reason. Transfer the special watch from the floor of the main hall to the flying controls laboratory. I'll set up the other side of the thing with Old. And George,' I went on, 'there's a metallurgy lab on the second floor, isn't there? Better put a guard on that, too.'

'I should love to know what you're up to.'

'Trust me, George.'

'I've no reason not to. But I do carry the can for security; can't you tell me what's going on?'

'I'm going fishing, George, using a red herring bait.'

I sank my sixth pint in the saloon of the Anglers Arms, and squinted across at Armstrong. 'You were bloody right, my old mate.'

It was ten o'clock on Saturday evening and the place was crowded. Anyone with flapping ears would have no trouble getting close enough to hear, and I was sure Lovegrove would have someone there. He had sat tight for twenty-four hours, despite knowing for certain that his share dealings had been uncovered, and regardless of the situation in Number Five building where the elevator circuit had been taken away and set up under close guard in the laboratory. Some of its parts were under the microscope in the metallurgy section. I wanted Lovegrove to think I was close to having him as an accessory to murder, but he wasn't playing. As a last resort, I was using Armstrong's interest and my considerable capacity for alcohol to try and draw him out.

'How was I bloody right, old cock?' Armstrong was more than matching my consumption. He was sober enough to be stacking it all away in his reporter's brain. I hoped he was busy enough doing so to miss seeing that I was still sober.

'Big, dark, ugly story. More behind this one than we thought. Just like you said.' I made no great effort to keep my voice down.

'Daft. Dying a death, this thing.' If Armstrong really believed that he wouldn't have been there. 'We'll end up thinking the pilot's ticker gave out after all.'

MacPherson looked at each of us in turn. I dearly wanted

to glance around and see who was within earshot, but dared not.

'So *you* say.' I blinked and leaned forward. 'But you don't know what I've found.'

'What have you found?'

'A little something.'

'Is she nice?'

'Oh, funny.' I sank another half-pint at one go. Was there no way we could have strung one another along and stayed sober? 'I've found a little something that tells me John Rose couldn't hold the nose down on finals.'

'And what's that, then?' There was a note of challenge in his voice which was intended to make me blurt out the rest.

'Never you mind. Got the lab boys on to it, I have. I'll tell Bates when it's all sorted out. *And* Simpson,' I said with feeling.

'Who? Bates and Simpson?'

'Not *them*.' I allowed the scorn to add power to my voice. 'The bastards who...'

'Who what?' MacPherson slipped it in because I had stopped and Armstrong hadn't prodded me.

'Never mind that. I'm getting it all signed, sealed and delivered. Me, Neil Goddard. We'll show Morlands not to come over so high and bloody mighty.'

'You mean they were holding out on you?'

'I didn't say that.' Another pint appeared like magic beside me. I wondered if Armstrong would have the nerve to carve a story out of what I was saying. 'You can think what you like. But I'm holding out on *them*, my life I am.'

'You can't do that, old man.'

'Just watch me. It'll come to the same thing in the end, but for the sake of forty-eight hours I can have the credit instead of that shower over there. Oh hell, I've got to leave you.'

I left them, and took a stroll round the village. I needed to clear my head and give things a chance to happen.

He sat in the armchair in the corner of my room. I'd never seen him before, but I knew why he'd come and waited

60

with interest to see what line he would take. It would have to be moderately clever, for he could hardly take me out of the Anglers Arms at gunpoint. The sounds of revelry were building to a climax downstairs. I blinked at him and permitted myself an artistic sway. 'Who the hell are you? Get out.'

'You don't know me ...' he started.

'I know I don't know you. Get out.'

'I've something of interest to you, Mr Goddard.'

'No you haven't. Get lost, I'm going to bed.'

'It's orange,' he said with a slight air of desperation, 'about a foot and a half long and a foot round.'

'Then take it to Morlands. They'll know what to do with it. And with you.'

'I thought you'd help me!'

'Oh, really?'

'How can I go to Morlands?' He was painting a nice picture of himself as a wretched little unfortunate. 'I don't like it, see? They told me to pick this thing up and they paid me plenty. But they didn't say the aeroplane was going to come down on top of me, near as dammit, and they didn't say they were going to leave me sitting on it this long.'

'Poor you. Cracking under the strain, are you?' He was small and shabby, raincoated and brown-shoed, but not stupid. I leaned back against the wardrobe, shifting it under my weight.

'It's not been touched.'

'I should hope not. Got it at home, have you?'

'Down in Barnsdale. What can I do with it? I don't like it, Mr Goddard, and I don't know what to do. They got me into this and left me lumbered. They're up to something nasty, I know that now, but I helped them, didn't I? It's not something I can say to the police, is it? Or to Morlands.'

'You nasty little man.' I glared at him with distaste, trying to look as though I was going to take him apart. 'You saw the thing crash, but you stopped to pick up the recorder just the same, didn't you? They *told* you what would happen, didn't they?'

'So they did! So they did!' He was painfully aware of

being a foot shorter than me and five stone lighter. 'But they didn't say how close it would come. I swear I didn't know anyone would get killed. I thought the pilot had bailed out, that's what they said would happen.'

'You little clown.' Despite my inner satisfaction at having made contact, my temper was rising. 'Who's got the other one, then?'

'Other one?' His face was a moon of stupefaction. I knew then that he hadn't been anywhere near the crash.

'Never mind. Are you going to bring it here?' Like hell he would, he was the bait for the trap. It was a pretty transparent trap, they must be reckoning on my being drunk as hell. Either that, or they knew what I knew; that I couldn't afford to turn down the chance of getting at them.

'Not on your life,' he said. 'I'll not be seen carrying t'bloody thing about, not no more. Like I said, you don't know me. I'll give it thee if you come now. You can take it away, and you still won't know me. You'll have what you want then, won't you? And you'll have to leave me out of it, because you'll not find me again.'

'I'm sure you'll disappear easier than most,' I said.

He ignored the jibe and rose, not without satisfaction. 'You'll come now? I'll not give you another chance, see? I can't trust thee to keep it to thysen.' He wasn't local, either; he had the accent right, but his grammar was letting him down.

'If I wanted to pull you in, little man,' I said with dignity, 'I could do it now, couldn't I?' Yes, but what good would a minion be? He wouldn't be able to tell us anything, but if I let him go, the lead would go with him. 'Come on,' I said roughly. I would just have to keep my eyes open, and seek to preserve a way out.

Barnsdale was a gleam of wet, dead roads, a succession of ugly terraced house fronts and factory walls. A place of dirt and dashed hopes. My companion drove round in circles until he was confident I was lost, a confidence I shared. It was a miracle to me that the car kept going. He had a battered Morris Minor, heaterless and gutless, which fitted his projected personality but had probably been borrowed for the occasion.

He stopped in a chasm of Victorian architecture, the narrow façades frowning down from both sides. The street lighting would have been terrible even if all the lamps had been working. The local council had lovingly plastered second-rate tarmac over random sections of the original cobblestones.

'Come in,' he said, 'and I'll get it for thee.'

'Nothing doing. You fetch it out, I'll wait here.'

He glared at me for a moment, shrugged his shoulders and climbed out of the car. Had they really expected me to be that daft? He vanished through the front door of the house, taking the car keys with him. If he thought that helped, he was wrong. I pulled the wires from behind the ignition switch by their roots, and twisted the ends together. The warning lamps glowed on the dashboard. The car was so old that the starter was a separate button.

As I moved across into the driving seat, there was a stir from the next doorway. An interlocked couple came swaying out of the pitch darkness and wandered past the car, passionately unaware of my presence. I looked away, and saw a much more interesting pair of newcomers making their way towards me from the end of the street. There was something purposeful about the way they moved, and they were both big. I waited until they had passed through two isolated pools of light, and decided I didn't like the look of them at all. The starter whirred as I hit the button.

The two men broke into a run, confirming my fears, and I kept my thumb on the starter and my eyes on them. That was a mistake. The car door opened and before I could turn round, it all went dark. I shouldn't have taken the lovers at face value.

# ◢12◣

I was blind. My eyes were wide open, yet there was nothing but inky blackness. I waited for it to clear while the rest of my senses came crawling back, but my vision did not join them. My memory sorted itself out sufficiently to carry me through the car ride and their neat diversionary tactics. The whole thing had been organised by someone with brains and people.

I lay on my back. My fingers explored the bare boards, moved up to the pillow beneath my neck and then the plaster patch behind my ear. At least they had done something to repair their handiwork, so presumably they hadn't finished with me. I held my hand just in front of my face and flexed the fingers to and fro, and still saw nothing. When I hauled myself to a sitting position there was a stab of pain at the back of my neck, but not enough to knock me out again.

Five minutes later I had painstakingly built up a partial picture, by feel alone. My bed—bench, rather—fitted snugly across the end of some kind of cellar. Three of the walls were brick, with no sign of a window. They were filthy to the touch, dusty and dry. The fourth boundary of my existence was a set of vertical bars, well embedded in concrete at the floor and in the brick arch above. There was a door, just a section of the bars cut out and set on hinges. It was massively locked.

Once I was convinced that there was nothing wrong with my eyes except a very efficient blackout, I cheered up slightly. It was encouraging that I had provoked them into rash action. Already I had an idea how many people Love-

grove had involved. There were six at least; my original
little man, the one who had opened the door of the house
to him, the two men who had come down the street to
hold my attention and the two who had actually got me.

What did he hope to gain by it all? Perhaps he just
wanted me out of the way while he took steps to dispose
of the evidence he thought I had found. What would happen when he found there *was* no evidence? In a way, now
they had done this, I myself counted as evidence. I had
stuck my neck out way beyond the call of an AIB inspector's
duty, and I hoped somebody would miss me soon. They
had taken my watch, so I had no idea what time it was. It
looked as though I might be in for a spot of mild brain-
washing.

There was a sound, a creaking of hinges. I strained my
eyes, but still there was no glimmer of light, not the least
crumb of comfort for my optic nerves. I relaxed on my
bench and waited to see what happened next.

A door slammed, and I heard footsteps and breathing.

'Goddard, I know you're awake now.'

An educated voice with the merest trace of Barnsdale.
He would be on the far side of the bars, feeling his way
just as I had done. There must be another darkened room
beyond, a sort of light-lock so that he could slip in without
breaking the stygian gloom. I said nothing.

'You moved, Goddard, and you're not the sort of man to
suffer a relapse. If you're hoping I'll come in there and
prod you so that you can grab me, forget it.'

'I never knew you cared.' If he had heard me moving,
they must have a microphone in the cellar.

'Ah, *that's* better. If you can raise a funny answer you
can't be feeling too bad. Let's get down to business, shall
we?'

'Whose business?' I tried without success to place the
voice. The darkness made it all too easy to imagine any
sort of face behind his floating, even-tempered words.

'My employer's business. He is worried, Goddard.'

'That was the idea.'

'You appear to have stumbled across his, er, guilty secret.'
He gave no sign of resenting my interruption or making

anything of it. I hoped it would sink in deeper if there was somebody listening on the microphone. 'What did you find, Goddard, and who have you told?'

'It's *his* guilty secret. He should know what I've found.'

'Don't fool, Goddard. This will go on as long as it has to.'

'Within limits. How long do you think I can go missing?'

'Long enough. Morlands think you are back with AIB. They won't exactly scream for you to come back.'

'And what do you hope to gain?' It was something of a blow, that; my own fault for playing the lone wolf too much.

'We were firmly under the impression, Goddard, that there was nothing to give the game away in the wreckage of the President. We have looked as well as we can, and we still do not know what *you* have found. Once we know that, we can take steps to safeguard ourselves.'

'You think it's as easy as that?' Somehow I had to get out of them a line on how it had been done.

'I'm not sure I know what you mean, Goddard.'

'It's not just a matter of running off with a few bits of aeroplane. You'd have to destroy all the photographs as well, not to mention making sure that none of the people concerned ever say a word. That includes me, of course.'

'You're not very well placed to point that out, Goddard.' It sounded all the more menacing because he made no attempt to make it sound so. 'As for all those others, it doesn't tie in with what you were saying in the Anglers Arms, does it? When you were in your cups, you were going to keep the honour and glory of finding the solution all to yourself.'

'I've told everybody who needs to know about everything I've found in that wreckage.' It was literally true, and I had no trouble making it sound convincing.

'That's bad, Goddard. You gave them your conclusions as well as your findings?'

'And what else should I do?'

'How many people now know exactly why the President crashed?'

'I've no idea.' We were working up to a crisis point. I only wished I could see his face.

'Morland? Bates? Simpson?' He cast around the obvious group.

'I've no idea,' I repeated.

'What?'

'The only people who know how it was done are the people who did it. I presume you're one.'

'Goddard, if you are seeking the limits of my patience...'

'You idiot. Have you not realised how you were provoked into making a move when none was needed? I made you think I'd found something in the elevator control circuit, right? And you panicked, just as I hoped.'

'It's not got you very far, has it?' He sounded like a man saying one thing and thinking something else, and not as worried as I would have liked. 'If you're right and there *is* no evidence, you've very little to go on.'

'You're giving me more evidence all the time. And the police won't need much to go on.'

'The police? Goddard, you're not serious!' He was so relieved he was almost laughing. 'You think Morland will have the police in on this thing? He's in enough trouble with his board and shareholders as it is.'

'If you're that confident,' I said, 'shut up and fade away.'

'Yes, I really think that might be the answer.'

'You won't do it without making sure I told the truth, will you?' I couldn't afford to have him take me at my word.

'I wouldn't dream of it, Goddard, I assure you.' That was nice, because if he faded away at once I would have nothing to go on. If he checked some more, it achieved two things; more time for me, more risk for him.

The sound of the door slamming woke me from a fitful sleep into the chill darkness.

'Goddard!' came the voice, hard with anger.

'What's come over you? You were supposed to have faded by now. Go away.' I was hungry as hell.

'What sort of fools did you think we were?' My ears hadn't deceived me, he was extremely cross. 'We know what tests they are running in the laboratory.' Running tests? That was more than I knew myself. 'What gave it to you, Goddard?' he went on. 'What put you on to the explosion?'

'Explosion?' It caught me so unawares that I sounded stupid. He was on to it like a flash, but he drew entirely the wrong conclusion.

'Don't try fooling me again, Goddard. You did it once, I'll not stand for it again. The explosion, the cutting of the elevator control rods. What gave you the idea? What did you find, who did you tell?'

He wasn't a technical man, for he sounded as though he had learned some of his lines parrot-fashion. I would have taken long odds he didn't know what an elevator control rod was, and for the first time I doubted the quality of the opposition. Besides, the whole thing was nonsense. 'There was no explosion,' I said baldly.

'Talk sense, Goddard. It was our explosion, and we know that you know.'

'There *was* no explosion.' I had to repeat myself, not only to get the message across but to stop him sounding like a music-hall act.

'It crashed where it was supposed to, yet you try to tell me our device didn't work?'

I was no longer thinking at my best, though a glimmer of light was beginning to dawn. 'Had you cut the control rods,' I explained, 'the power control units would have failed to the centre position. Not only would the aircraft have behaved differently; a pilot as good as John Rose might have held it on the trimmer alone. Apart from that, the whole elevator control run is just aft of the flight deck, there could have been no explosion without the crew hearing it. They would have reported *that* if it was the last thing they did. Yet there was nothing, no suggestion of anything like that.'

The silence was complete. His thinking was now chasing mine along a new path. If their device had failed, why had the President crashed? I was so used to accepting the unlikely by then that I had an answer before he could gather himself for another bluster. 'You were outsmarted,' I said. 'Somebody else did something *very* clever and left you to shoulder the blame, if we ever discovered anything. I wonder what they could have done?'

'It bears thinking about, Goddard.' He sounded understandably shaken. 'I shall have to take advice.' If his adviser was listening in on the microphone, he wouldn't have far to go.

'He should know enough to tell you I'm right,' I said, 'even though it was a cockeyed scheme he dreamed up.'

'You'd better be right, Goddard.' He was back to bluster.

'Listen, this is important.' I tried to imagine him, there in the darkness. 'Whoever it was used as much of your scheme as they could; used your wiring, perhaps, but did away with your little bomb. They knew all about *you*. But I'm not interested in you any more; only them. You didn't achieve anything, whatever your intentions, but you may have a line on the others. Give me a lead, and I'll leave you alone.'

'As I said once before,' came the reply, 'you're poorly placed to bargain.' The door slammed.

After so long in utter darkness, the light woke me more quickly than a kick in the ribs would have done. I blinked into the beam and wondered why I couldn't get up. There was a jangle and scrape at the door in the bars and the light came closer. It left my face and travelled the length of me, a probing pencil beam, and then flashed sideways to cover the walls. The dim reflection from the filthy brick betrayed the shape behind the torch, and I knew this was my last chance. In a few more hours I would be physically so far gone that I wouldn't be able to lift a finger. As the shape came closer I lunged suddenly, but succeeded only in rolling off the bench and crashing heavily to the floor.

I didn't quite pass out, but it was as much as I could do to sit there and breathe heavily. The shape crouched down beside me and spoke for the first time.

'It *is* Mr Goddard, isn't it?' Beyond the fact that it was a female voice, it didn't register, though it seemed remarkably confident considering the dark and the surroundings. 'You're in a mess, you are. Can you stand up?'

I could, but only with difficulty. I needed some help

from my new-found friend. Walking was another matter altogether. We managed a couple of steps at a time but it took an age to get out to a room with some natural light, and there wasn't much of that, just a gaslight glimmer through a filthy basement window. I wasn't seeing very clearly, and my body felt as though it didn't belong to me.

'Are you hurt anywhere, Mr Goddard?' she was saying. By listening hard, I could just make sense of it. I shook my head and leaned on her. She hardly wilted under the strain, which said a lot for her strength. It was dawning on me that I had been without food or water for some time, but one loses strength before weight. We pressed on, but the stairs were a nightmare. I flopped on the first landing.

'Water,' I croaked. My tongue was swollen and difficult to control but she caught on. It was the dehydration that had done the real damage; anyone my size can starve for some time without suffering more than a weakness at the knees.

She seemed to be gone a long time, so long that I even got round to wondering who she was. When she came back she had a mug brim-full of water. Afterwards she admitted finding it in a tank outside the back door, but in my state the quality didn't matter. I gulped the stuff down and for a moment it was marvellous, then the pain hit me in the stomach and I doubled up with a groan of agony. It took some time for the pain to die down and after that I was able to unfold myself and move faster, but my head was swimming and I was no longer able to keep track of what was happening. It was my own fault; having remembered half my desert survival lectures I had forgotten the other half, and she wasn't to know.

The next time I woke up, things had taken a turn for the better. It was warmer and brighter and softer, and I lay back and felt a proper bed under my weakness. Then my memory began to work overtime and I croaked something wicked and tried to sit up.

The single, gentle hand which appeared had no trouble pushing my head back on the pillow. I looked round cautiously to see where it had come from. She was sitting beside the bed, and this time I recognised the young reporter from the local paper.

'How do you feel, Mr Goddard?' Her voice and face were serious, and her brown eyes searched my face.

'Better than I should. How did you do it?'

'Carefully.' She smiled. 'You nearly passed out after I fetched you that water, remember? When I got you here I spent a long time squeezing water down your throat from a cloth, drop by drop. That seemed to suit you better, so I tried it with some sugar solution, and added a bit of salt for good measure.'

'That wasn't a bad idea.'

'I'm not daft, you know. We do have a reference library where I work.'

'Oh, yes.' I lay and worried about the implications of where she worked.

'Hell,' I said, because daylight was creeping past the drawn curtains, 'what time is it?'

'Half past eight.'

'I'm sorry. I mean, what day is it?'

'Wednesday.' She looked a good deal more anxious.

'Christ!' I had been out of circulation since Saturday night. She must have nursed me through the last few hours, so I had been nearly three days in that blasted cellar. This time she didn't stop me when I sat up and looked around. It was a narrow, tight little bedroom, all patterned wallpaper and second-hand furniture. 'Why didn't you take me to hospital?' I asked.

'I wasn't sure you'd want to be taken to hospital.' She withdrew slightly into a mantle of dignity. 'There was nothing much wrong with you that I could see, and I didn't know what sort of mess I'd be stirring up if I dumped you there.'

'That worried you?' I made the alarming discovery that she had shaved me while I slept. Perhaps she had wanted to make sure it really was me. There was a new plaster under my chin to match the one behind my ear.

'It worried me quite a lot,' she confessed, and I realised she was talking about the hospital and not the shave. 'I

71

know why you came to Barnsdale, after all; who you are and what you're trying to do. I've a legitimate interest in what's going on. But then you'd not remember me, would you?' For a moment I didn't see what she was driving at.

'Oh, yes I do. You're the number two reporter from the *Barnsdale and District Gazette and Herald*.'

'Actually it's the *Barnsdale Echo*. And I'm the number three reporter.'

'How many reporters do they have?'

'Three.' Her face stayed frozen but there was humour somewhere behind it. 'They never introduced us, did they? I'm Jean Partington.'

'I still don't know why you kept me clear of the hospital, Jean.'

'Because you're up to something.'

'Like what?'

'*I* don't know, but either you've a reason for the way you're carrying on, or you're a disgrace. You were shouting your head off in the Anglers Arms, by all accounts, and it's not like you.'

'How would you know it's not like me?'

'It just isn't.' Beneath any woman's intelligence you find a foundation of intuition. I was glad it had been denied to Lovegrove's minions. 'Then,' Jean went on, 'there was the way I found you.'

'And how was that?'

'We had a telephone call to the office.'

'Telling the news desk there was something interesting in a certain cellar.'

'Had they done that, we'd have passed the message straight on to the police. No; they asked for me and told me I'd find an exclusive to do with the Morlands crash. So I took the risk and went.'

'Of course, you couldn't throw away the chance of an exclusive, could you?'

She stood up and walked towards the window before turning to face me. 'I do wish you wouldn't make it sound that way,' she said, but I had the feeling she was fighting down anger. 'I'm mixed up in this thing so many ways ... anybody local is,' she finished lamely. 'Not like all those aviation specialists who came rushing up from London.'

'You seemed to get on well enough with one or two of them.'

'You've no right to say that.' She coloured slightly. 'They knew much more about aeroplanes than I did. I had to learn from them to get my own story straight.'

'Great. Brought up in the shadow of Morlands and you don't know a damn thing about aeroplanes. Did you fill in MacPherson on the local background so that he could get *his* story straight?'

'You bastard,' she said in a voice of crystal clarity. 'One more clever answer and I'll pitch you out to fend for yourself.' The light from the window behind turned her hair into a soft brown halo. I realised for the first time how tall she was; five foot eight or nine. She had the firm chin and wide-set eyes which so many of the nicer Yorkshire girls seem to inherit. I felt ashamed, and she'd hardly started.

'I've looked after you all night,' she said, 'and told the paper nothing. They'll not thank me for that. I don't give a damn what you think, I want to do what's best for this town and that means helping you finish whatever you've started. Morlands means a lot to the people of Barnsdale. It's a job for many of them, my father included...'

'Just a moment, Jean.' The name clicked into place. 'I'm sorry; being clever has come to be a habit with me. Your father is superintendent in Number Five, isn't he? Bert Partington?'

'That's right.' The anger had gone. 'I didn't know you knew him.'

'He never mentioned me?'

'He *never* talks about his job. Least of all to me.' I had a vision of Bert in a quandary about his journalist daughter.

'I shouldn't have said any of that, Jean. I see it all now.'

'Never mind that, Mr Goddard.'

'Neil.'

'Neil, what was going on? Off the record,' she said with a smile, 'I know it has to be. What did you find? Why did they keep you there? And why did they then let you go?'

'I didn't find anything,' I confessed. 'Three days ago, I thought they were on the run; now I'm right back to square one.' I tried sliding bits of it into place, but parts of my memory were hazy. It was difficult to remember exactly what had gone on, what had been said. 'Jean,' I said, 'I have to take a good look at the place where you found me. Can you take me there?'

'Of course I can. But not until you've had something to eat, or you'll just pass out on me again.'

As soon as we turned into the street, I remembered. In the daylight it looked meaner still, and I could see that many of the houses were unoccupied, their windows boarded up like blind eyes. Paint daubs showed where the electricity had been cut off.

'It's not a nice part of town, this,' said Jean. 'Most of these people are being moved out to new flats. In a year or two they'll be along with the bulldozers and have the whole area flat, ready for a new shopping centre or something.' We reached the house, and she turned the front door handle. I looked up and down the street, but nobody was watching.

Inside, the house was like a museum of distemper and wallpaper, with the last exhibits added twenty years ago.

'At least it's dry,' I said. 'I was glad of that.'

'It's no reason not to be. We're up towards Newton Hill here, a long way above the river. This would have been a nice house once, in the middle of the last century. For a mill foreman, maybe, or a small merchant. Narrow, but deep; three floors up, basement below, cellar below that, where I found you.'

'A nice place, and the front door opens on to the street?'

'You try gardening in our weather. Besides, nothing'd grow.' She smiled at me and led the way downstairs. 'It'll be a mess now,' she called over her shoulder. 'Fifty year old electric wiring and a cat's-cradle of gas and water pipes; not worth the bother of putting straight.'

'It'd be worth a fortune in London.'

'I dare say.' Jean dismissed London.

They had done such a good job of clearing out that I began to worry that they'd not played the game. Probably there hadn't been much to clear out, it would have been a purely temporary hideout. The police might have had fun

74

looking for fingerprints but the voice from the dark had been right; nobody wanted a lot of fuss with the police at this stage, least of all me. Jean and I worked our way from cellar to top floor without finding anything that made sense.

'Are you expecting to find anything?' asked Jean as we stood dustily in the attic.

'Definitely. Either that, or somebody's going to be sorry.'

She frowned at me and had the good sense not to ask for an explanation. 'There's a sort of loft,' she said.

We found them in the loft: two orange cylinders, a foot wide and eighteen inches long, with an envelope taped to one of them. I slipped it open and found a neat electrical circuit diagram. Jean peered over my shoulder and I remembered who her father was.

'What are they?' She stared at the cylinders and prodded at one with a neat foot.

'Jean? Did you mean what you said, about helping me get to the bottom of all this?'

'Did you think I was joking?'

'No. But now, I have to be sure.'

'Why, Neil? What are these things?'

'Crash recorders.'

'From the Morland crash? What are they doing here?' I could see her thoughts chasing mine down the same route, and I have to admit she was quicker. 'The people who kept you here, Neil. They took them, didn't they? And if they took them, they must have...'

'Actually, no. They thought they'd crashed the President—'

'President?'

'That's what they've called the aircraft. Listen; these people *thought* they'd done it, but while they were grilling me we tumbled to the fact that someone else had done better still. So we did a sort of deal; if they told me what they'd tried to do, I'd leave them alone.'

'And this is their way of doing it? It's lucky they still had the recorders.'

'Not really. The things are virtually indestructible, they'd

75

have been a nightmare to get rid of. Easier by far to hide them somewhere safe.'

'I see. What are you going to do now?'

'I'll have to take these up to Morlands. After that, I've some designing to do.'

'Designing?'

'I have to start with this,' I said, waving the electrical drawing, 'and turn it into something much more sure and subtle.' It was going to be a problem. 'These people were completely out-thought by somebody else.'

'Neil?'

'Yes, Jean?'

'You will be more careful from now on, won't you?'

# ◢13◣

Simpson came in and looked at the sheets of paper strewn over my desk. 'Not working out?' He admired my uninspired scrawls and gazed at the pile of President electrical system drawings.

'It has to work out somehow, George.' One of the people in the successful plot must be a first-class electrician.

'Bert Partington tells me he's sorted out the parts you were specially interested in. Coming to have a look?'

'Coming.' I picked up the pile of system drawings and followed him downstairs.

Bert had sifted out all the switches and wiring looms, setting them all up on a separate frame. My main interest was in the automatic microswitches. In effect, these are electrical interlocks which ensure that when something happens—when the flaps or wheels come down, or the aircraft touches down—various other things automatically follow suit. For instance, the pilot of the President didn't have to cancel the flap blowing and put out the air brakes when he landed, the microswitches did it all for him. The President systems used them a great deal; Bert had rescued twelve all told, complete with their tangles of wiring.

'I've found nothing wrong,' he said by way of greeting. 'Such as we have, it checks out. Of course, there are lots of places where the wiring is no longer continuous, but I've not found a mistake yet.'

'You've made specially sure of the flap blowing microswitch?' I said. Lovegrove's bunglers—I no longer felt anything but sorry for Lovegrove—had arranged their little surprise packet to explode when the flap blowing was switched on below five thousand feet. They had wired it through one of the height interlocks so that when John had tried the blowing at a nice safe ten thousand feet, nothing had happened. Yes; but somebody had been more cunning still, had taken out their tiny bomb and arranged instead that the President should destroy itself.

'I know it sounds silly, Bert,' I said, fingering the vital microswitch, 'but are we sure this is the same one that came in with the wreckage in the first place?'

'We'll soon check,' he said, looking at me hard. We trooped across to his office, a roomy place with one wall formed entirely of box files. He searched for ten seconds or so, selected one and brought it across. Inside were photographs of a particular section of crash fragments, the microswitch included. He took several of them, and we went back to compare. There was no doubt about it, the pictures tallied with the switch as closely as anyone could tell, and the switch was wired up exactly as the drawing in my hand said it should be.

'Carry on checking, Bert,' I said wearily. 'See if you can find any identification tags on the wires changed round. They would have had to do that to cover up any fiddling.' Aircraft wiring doesn't come in pretty colours like the loom in a car; it is all high-temperature stuff, and you sort out one wire from another by its identifying sleeve.

'I don't understand it,' I confessed to George Simpson as we walked away. 'Whatever was done, it didn't show up in

77

the ground checks before the first flight. Was it so clever that it wouldn't have shown, or did they do it at the very last moment?'

'Search me, old boy. Why can't we find it now, that's what I want to know? Let's see how they're getting on with your crash recorders.' The recorders were a sore point with George, because I wouldn't tell him where they had come from.

They were getting on very well, transferring the signals on the magnetic tapes into visible traces on long rolls of paper. Bates looked up as we came in.

'I'm glad to see you back, wherever you've been.'

'Only for what I've brought with me.' I smiled back at him. Could it be Bates? He had the technical expertise to organise it. I was aware of a tendency on my part to suspect everyone, even to speculate how old Morland might have done it, and why. The question of motive was the trickiest of all. Lovegrove had been in it for gain—to clear off his debts—but the man I was looking for now had a more subtle object.

'Look at this.' Bates was blissfully unaware of my thoughts. 'It's crazy.' I looked over his shoulder. He was exaggerating, it simply confirmed what we knew already. All the time the President had been nosing fatally high, the elevator angle trace showed an increasing value, as though John had been deliberately pulling her higher still. It made no sense at all. 'I can't hold her...' If that last desperate transmission meant anything, it was that John was shoving hard forward on the wheel and had the trim switch jammed forward into the bargain. Yet the elevator had kept on moving up. I was reminded of my words in the press conference, when I had said the recorders wouldn't add anything; I had been right.

'What's that?' I pointed into the President's flying control ground test rig, a monster frame which held the controls just as they ran in the aircraft.

'Gearing unit,' said Bates tersely. 'We have to vary the amount of elevator movement according to conditions. At low speed, we need a lot of movement; if we allowed that much at high speed the pilot could tear the aircraft to pieces.'

'Wouldn't that normally be part of the artificial feel unit?'

'It would, except that we're using our own units, much simpler ones. All part of our drive on cost—and secrecy.'

'How is the gearing switched?'

'Full movement when the wheels are down. Two-thirds below three hundred knots. One-third above that.'

'All done with microswitches?'

'That's right.'

I turned at a movement beside me, and found Arthur Morland standing at my elbow, the hangar lights catching his fair hair.

'Seen the recorder traces?' he asked. 'John Rose was pulling the thing into a climb all the time. It's what I said, he must have had a seizure or something.'

'Not necessarily.' It was Bates who spoke, angrily.

'Oh, really, Bates! I'm surprised at *you* wandering about looking for systems failures that never happened. We can't stop AIB doing it if they want to, but we should be concentrating on clearing that second aircraft.'

I looked at Arthur Morland, wondering whether he was technically capable enough, and morally bad enough, to have set the whole thing up with the aim of landing the Chief Test Pilot's job. Reluctantly, I decided he was neither. 'What's all this about the second aircraft?' I asked.

The question was for Bates but it was young Morland, in his eagerness, who replied. 'She was wheeled out yesterday for first engine runs. They went very well. I'll be flying her next week, if the rest of the schedule works out the same way.'

'I really wouldn't do that.' It wasn't much of a stand but I had to make it. Morland took a step back and looked me up and down, every inch the boss's son.

'Look here, Goddard. It's about time we sorted this out. It was made plain enough to you that you were up here on sufferance. It is no part of your job to try and obstruct the rest of our programme. Your *official* terms of reference concern the fate of the first aircraft only. Really, I wonder whether your attitude isn't part of the whole damned Ministry plot to see us out of the aircraft business.'

Bates shuffled uncomfortably.

'Arthur,' I said companionably, 'if that's how you talk when you're sober, I hope they don't let you out when you're drunk.'

'How dare you!' Morland's face changed colour very quickly.

'What you said just then was actionable, if I cared to take it that way.' I was sufficiently annoyed to forget who might be within earshot. 'That's one point. For another, you'd do well to behave more responsibly unless you fancy the Ministry asking for the return of your licence. And for a third, I could always block the flight by requesting a temporary withdrawal of Morlands' ARB design approval.'

Arthur Morland's face worked its way from pink astonishment to crimson rage without regaining the power of speech. He turned abruptly on his heel and stormed off without a word.

'He's gone to see his old man now,' warned Bates. 'I know he wants leaning on, but you bloody near drove him into the ground.'

'I'm sorry, Brian.' Bates deserved my sympathy, not to mention my thanks. He knew much better than Arthur the job I'd have persuading the ARB to disavow Morlands, even as a temporary expedient, but he had let it ride. 'That wasn't meant for you,' I confessed. 'Let's try sorting the thing out properly. Can we set it up on the simulator—the second aircraft, even—and see what happens?'

'Certainly.' For Brian, my outburst might never have happened. 'I'll lay you long odds, though, that we find nothing. All this was part of the test schedule for the first aircraft, and look what happened. It's infuriating, isn't it,' he said gloomily, 'to think that the answer is in there somewhere.' We looked at the controls sliding back and forth on the rig, and still the answer escaped me.

'I hear you've been setting yourself up as our new Managing Director,' said Sir William Morland.

'It depends who you've been listening to. I had to remind Arthur that his priorities didn't necessarily coincide with mine. He wants nothing more than to be the first man to land a President in one piece.'

'That's as may be. D'you have good reason to deny him? Let me remind you of your record to date, Goddard. You've wandered off without reference to anyone and reappeared with the crash recorders, yet you'll not tell us where or how you found them...' He gave me a chance to say something, then pressed on as I remained silent. 'Even now, we're no nearer arriving at a reason for the crash. Do you still tell me we should hold the second flight?'

'Yes, I do. *Because* we've found no reason. We don't know how it was done, but it certainly failed to show up in any pre-flight check on the aircraft. The least we can do is be a damned sight more clever checking the second one before we let it fly.'

'And the tighter security? With the new guard on Number Five, could they even have got at the second aircraft?'

'That depends how it was done. Suppose it was organised in the drawing office? The man who built the fatal flaw into the first aircraft may have done it in all good faith, working to a drawing.'

'Then we'll check the drawings, every last one of them.'

'Bates is seeing to it now. Though I don't hold out any great hope.'

'Could they cover their tracks so well?'

'They might not have to. Suppose they're confident we won't spot what they've done?'

'Keep at it, lad.' Morland made a face. 'They'll make a mistake eventually. Let's hope they do it before the second flight.'

'If they don't,' I said, 'if we can't find anything in either drawings or aircraft, there's one thing I'd like to ask.'

'What's that?'

'The right hand seat in the second aircraft.'

'Fly it with Arthur? Is that all?'

'Now look.' I was deadly serious. 'I've no certain way of stopping 02. I could try, but the most likely result would

81

be a sharpening of the Ministerial chopper. So I'm asking you to keep Arthur and your board in check for the time being. If you can't or won't, the least you can do is let me be on hand.'

'You think Arthur will wear it?'

'He will, if you tell him he must.'

Morland chewed it over for a moment. 'Very well. I can't hold things up very long, you know. Come next week we'll have to fly it. Besides, could it be that the man behind all this may be relying on our reacting this way? That having destroyed the first aircraft, he has also destroyed our confidence to proceed? Remember what you were told right at the start; time is as vital to us as money.'

'Certainly. But look at it like this; if it was done in the workshops, they'd be mad to try it a second time. On the other hand, if it was done from the drawing office, they may not be able to *stop* it going on the second aircraft. That will have been built to the same drawings as the first.'

'I've known few people as optimistic as you, Goddard,' said Morland with ponderous wit. 'That's all for you and Bates to sort out between you. And Goddard; don't threaten me the way you threatened Arthur, not ever. I'm not above retaliation. I've my own notions about Arthur, don't think the boy's a blind spot where I'm concerned. He may not appreciate it, but he's working on a make-or-break basis these next few weeks. If it makes him, I'll be glad; but if it breaks him I'll not be sorry, you understand that?'

'Yes,' I said. 'I understand.'

'You'll get your ride beside him, don't worry. Though what your wife will think about it is another matter, and no concern of mine, thank God.'

Jean's flat was nicer the second time round. Her character was reflected in the living room: good books, typewriter on the cluttered desk, Beethoven sonata on an upright piano. One looked in vain only for an expression of her underlying hardness.

'Suppose something had gone up when it should have gone down,' I called to her through the bathroom door, 'why do you think it would have happened?'

'Somebody must have crossed a wire somewhere, I suppose.' Water gurgled from the basin.

'But it wouldn't have worked,' I protested. 'There are no wires in the main control circuit, just pushrods and hydraulic pressure.'

'Well, they must have switched something,' said Jean with stubborn common sense. 'Wires are easier to switch than anything else, aren't they?'

'Yes, but there's no way they could have done it. We've checked the drawings, the rig and the second aircraft.'

'That's wrong thinking, Neil.' The bathroom door opened. 'They *did* it,' she said. 'You're just not clever enough to see how. Try putting yourself in their position; how would *you* have done it?'

I should have listened harder at that moment but Jean was wearing a brown woollen dress that exactly matched her hair. I realised for the first time that her eyes were a very pale brown, almost yellow.

'You might have told me,' I said.

'Told you what?' Her smiling sideways tilt of the head was becoming a familiar gesture.

'That you could look like that. You're a public danger.'

'Stop it,' she said, 'before I start wondering whether you really mean it.'

The gaiety of the Anglers Arms had been little abated by the departure of most of the journalists. Jean and I wandered into the bar and if anything it seemed more crowded than usual, and noisier. Most of the laughter came from a crowd in one corner. I shrugged at Jean and steered her towards a table, and then by one of those strange trick movements the crowd split for a moment and I came to a grinding halt.

It would have been bad enough coming across one of the people I least wanted to meet in the whole wide world; instead I faced two of them. One was Arthur Morland, who was clearly playing host. The other was a small but perfect blonde whose blue eyes merely widened for a second before she rose.

She had a presence, part gift and part education, and the crowd fell back and quietened as she walked towards us. 'Neil, darling.' It was her crystal-clear actress voice, pitched to carry without effort to the corners of the bar. 'You told me it was a *dreadful* little place, and I think it's absolutely adorable.' She paused for effect, having achieved her object of an expectant hush. 'I've been waiting for you for ages, Neil,' she complained. 'If it hadn't been for Mr Morland bringing me from the factory I don't know what I would have done.'

I looked past her at Morland, who seemed suitably pleased with himself. 'I'm sorry,' I said, choking down a suggestion as to what she might have done. 'I had a few things to do down in Barnsdale. You should have let me know you were coming.'

'I'm sorry if I surprised you, darling.' She fed herself a cue to cast a sweeping glance at Jean. 'I know you've been working *very* hard.' She thrived on the breathless semi-silence just as I found it uncomfortable. The bar was full of people either listening or trying not to. At least Jean was equal to the situation.

'Hello, Mrs Goddard.' It must have been glaringly obvious, but Jean gave it a cool confidence which Liz should have taken as a warning. 'I'm Jean Partington of the *Barnsdale Echo*. Mr Goddard was looking through some of our files on Morland Aircraft's history.' That was an unblushing lie, she was trying to spare me an awkward situation.

'How interesting.' Liz made it sound as fascinating as last year's fashions. 'I'm sure you were a great help to him, my dear.' She might have been four years older than Jean, and looked younger, but she said it with the air of a dowager duchess addressing a first-season debutante. Jean flushed for the first time.

'We help as best we can,' she said, and the strain of anger contained showed in the richer hint of Barnsdale accent. 'Neil's work is very important for a lot of our people.'

Liz pounced. 'He lets you call him Neil! My dear, you *are* honoured. It took me simply ages to break him down that far.' Her smile was full of malice.

'Elizabeth,' I warned, but she was enjoying herself too much.

'He always calls me Elizabeth when he's cross,' she confided to Jean.

'Elizabeth,' I started again, 'just tell me two things.'

'Yes, darling?' Her expression was almost insultingly vacant. I sensed Morland drifting up behind her.

'Are you staying long, and how much have you had to drink?'

Liz had a trick of shifting from innocence to cold fury without moving a muscle of her face, and we were treated to a command performance. I didn't blame her, in fact I was banking on it, though it was hardly fair to Jean. The silence in the bar had become absolute, and I could hear Morland breathing heavily as he worked out what to say.

'You swine, Goddard.'

It was a disappointing start but I was denied a chance to comment, because Liz beat me to it.

'Shut up, Arthur.' She threw the remark over her shoulder with a proud toss of the head and turned back to me. 'You're a bastard, Neil. I come up here to help you and what do I find? You've been missing for three days, doing God knows what. You come wandering in here with the local newspaper girl hanging on your arm, and the best you can do is accuse me of being drunk and try to pack me off home again. Is that the best you can do for your wife?'

'The day you really come to help,' I said flatly, 'and stay off the drink until afterwards, then I'll apologise.'

Liz was too good an actress to splutter wordlessly. She looked at me as though I was beneath contempt, while Jean stood beside me like a pale statue.

'Liz,' said Arthur Morland pleadingly, 'it's not worth arguing with him in this mood. Come and have dinner at the Grange, we have more civilised company there.' The other inhabitants of the bar failed to take this as an insult, they merely regarded me as though I was letting them down.

We watched them go—Liz would never in a thousand

years have passed up a chance like that, and I had no wish to stop her—and Jean said she didn't much feel like dinner any more. It might have been better to book out of the place straight away, but in the end we simply drove back to Barnsdale, wandered around in silence for a bit and ended up in Jean's flat while she cooked us a meal.

'I'm sorry about all that,' I said eventually. Jean had made no comment for two hours.

'She's very lovely, Neil, isn't she?'

'She's clever, too. It's just that she's a dyed-in-the-wool bitch.' I had never confessed that to anybody before. 'Arthur Morland had better watch out; she'll run rings round him.' Jean nodded. 'Anyway,' I said, 'thank you for being so quick on the uptake, and for keeping your temper.'

'I wasn't really quick on the uptake, you know.' She gazed at me earnestly. 'You keep on forgetting my job, Neil. I went through your background very carefully when I was given the crash story to cover. I *knew* who she was, love. And I think you're being a bit hard on her.'

'Why so?'

'No, honestly. She has a lot to put up with in her own way, and she was never taught how to deal properly with someone like you.' Jean ploughed on through my rising protest. 'You're about the only person she can't charm into doing what she wants, don't you see that?'

'She charmed me into marrying her.'

'Don't be stupid, Neil! With looks like that, and the money to back it up, did you ever consider turning down the chance? Your bloody-mindedness was probably a big attraction for her then, but she's been regretting it ever since. Perversity isn't a very good foundation for a happy marriage.'

'You seem to know a lot about it.'

'I ought to.' Jean's face dissolved into a sudden smile. 'I do the paper's problem page.'

'My word! Dear Aunt Mary, what do you recommend?'

'Let her persuade you a bit more often. She'll be a lot happier, and you won't lose much. You're a bit of a stubborn cuss, you know.' The yellow eyes shone at me across the check tablecloth and the solitary candle.

86

It might have been good advice, but I should have spent more time listening to her talking about switching wires in the President.

Liz was waiting for me back at the hotel, and had clearly decided on contrition as the best approach. She said she was sorry until even I believed her, and finally I settled down and gave her an edited version of what had happened so far. I prayed that old Morland hadn't yet broken to Arthur the news of his replacement co-pilot, because if Liz was storing that up to break over my head I might as well go home.

'It was a political thing, then, sending you up here?' In so far as politics is the art of manipulating people, Liz took an interest in it.

'It was a political thing *asking* me up here. It enabled Morlands to fend off a lot of criticism.'

She snuggled against me. 'Couldn't you tell the office that Morlands are doing a grand job, and there's nothing you can do to help? Then we could go back to London. It's not a nice place, this.' She shivered prettily.

'You said you loved it, earlier this evening.'

'Not *this* place, silly. The whole area. If it isn't airfield it's coalmine, or canal or motorway. It's amazing that anywhere could have been made such a comprehensive mess, isn't it? Come back to London, Neil. You're getting nowhere up here, and it could be dangerous; I don't want to lose you, whatever I say in my darker tantrums.'

'Liz, I have to stay here a little while longer.' I recalled Jean's advice. 'We still don't know what's going on, but I've come as close to it as anybody. Don't you realise that Arthur Morland will fly the second aircraft next week regardless of whether we have found the cause of the first one crashing?'

'Arthur Morland.' She sniffed. It hadn't taken her long to fathom the new Chief Test Pilot. 'He hasn't grown up yet. Are we to be stuck up here until he's done his hero bit, and can we all go home after that?'

'We're stuck up here that long at least.'

'Oh,' she muttered in a tone which suggested she hadn't

87

yet given up. 'That girl,' she went on dreamily, 'she's quite nice, isn't she?'

'Quite nice, yes.' I avoided any feeling.

'In a *northern* sort of way, of course. I liked the way she backed you up and wouldn't say a word out of turn. Very loyal, I thought.'

'Bitch,' I said, but I should have been warned by the sudden loss of interest in returning to London. It was my night for misjudging women.

As it was, I thought no more of it until the Monday, by which time the second President had been checked all ways up and we were still no nearer a solution to the original problem.

The shock came when I was looking out over the Number Five apron at the aircraft's slender shape. They were towing it down to the detuner for final engine runs, after which Arthur would be able to start taxiing trials, perhaps on Wednesday. My chances of holding off the flight until the following week looked slim.

It came by special messenger, the small envelope with the AIB crest, and it contained no more than a curt summons. I was to leave Morlands to mind their own business; the office was short of people and a couple of incidents awaited urgent attention.

I rang Liz. 'They've recalled me,' I said baldly.

'What? Who have?' She sounded genuine, but six years had taught me that I never could tell for sure.

'The office. They want me down in London to look into some nasty little forced landing or other.'

'When shall we go?' She had spent the weekend lording it around the hotel, had been up to Morland Grange twice—to see Lady Morland, nothing to do with Arthur—and had even gone to church. I had been on the verge of believing she liked the place after all.

'We don't,' I said. 'You stay here and keep the hotel warm. Give Jean a ring on the *Echo*, she thinks you're not so bad really and she'll show you the rest of Barnsdale.'

'And what will you do?'

88

'I shall take a flying trip to London and find out what the hell is going on.'

'Oh, Neil! *Must* you fight it?'

'It stinks, that's why I'm going to fight it. I'll be back tomorrow.' And with that I asked the ground staff to wheel out the Piper. It would be quicker than the motorway, and my own car was parked at Biggin Hill.

'What's the matter, Neil? I didn't expect to find you down here in three hours flat.' Tony was his urbane self. 'It must be all that fresh Yorkshire air you've been getting.'

'It's fresher than the smell around here. When did you send off that recall?'

'Yesterday.'

'Yesterday was Sunday. Did things suddenly become so urgent that you rushed in here during the weekend to drag me back for a fresh start on Monday?'

'We needed you back here urgently, that's all. You're wasting your time up at Morlands; in two weeks of nosing around you've come up with nothing.'

'Haven't I, though?' I was rather too conscious of having kept Tony very much in the dark, especially about the crash recorder business, so I brought him up to date as rapidly as I could. He heard me out patiently and then set out to demolish me.

'My dear chap, you're still jumping to conclusions, aren't you? Let's accept that there was a sabotage attempt, which by the admission of those concerned failed to come off. Why should you at once conclude that there was another, successful attempt? It seems highly unlikely that two different plots would have been hatched to cripple the same aircraft. I understand the crash recorder shows signs of John Rose having been incapacitated.'

'Now who's jumping to conclusions? All we obtained from the crash recorder was a steady nose-up elevator movement, and that's a long way from saying there was anything wrong with the pilot. There's a lot I don't understand, beginning with the motive for the second sabotage plot. But somebody has to go looking for it or Morlands will have another disaster on their hands.'

'You pile one non-sequitur on another.' Tony sounded as though he was enjoying himself. 'What *proof* have you for the existence of your second plot? And why assume the second aircraft is in danger?'

'The only proof we have at the moment is that somebody neatly removed the tell-tale signs of the first plot without saying a word. Theirs was the better idea, and they didn't want an explosion giving the game away, so they took the bomb out of the elevator circuit and did something much more clever.'

'Has it not occurred to you that this bomb story might have been thought up to put you on the wrong track?'

'Yes, it did. I have to trust my own judgement, Tony; it sounded genuine the way it came across, and I think it was. The people I made contact with hadn't the wit to dream up a double-cross in that class. As for the second aircraft, my fear is that the fault is a paper one, that nothing physical has been done to the aircraft.'

'Designed-in, you mean?' Despite himself, Tony was interested.

'Sort of. And if it's been done that way, it will be in the second aircraft. Our problem is this; we can check all the drawings, given time, but we mustn't alarm people by doing it openly. And we don't *have* the time, because Morlands will have run out of excuses for not flying by some time this week.'

'That's their problem. You've done all you could.'

'I haven't, Tony, not by a long way. Can I talk to Mulligan?'

'You've no time for chewing over theories with an electrician. I need you down in Penzance today.'

'What the hell goes on in Penzance?'

'British Helicopters have lost an S61 down there.'

'Tony, mate.' He winced at my descent to gutter English. 'I'm not a helicopter man, right? You haul me off the Morlands business and send me about as far from Yorkshire as you can manage to tackle a job I'll do badly. What's the matter, have you forgotten the big make-or-break speech you gave me before I went up to Barnsdale? Have I simply not convinced you, or has somebody been getting at you?'

'That's enough.' He went all stiff on me. 'Let me remind you that you were sent to Morlands with a rather original brief: to convince people that the Ministry was taking a right and proper interest in the proceedings. As far as we can judge, you did that very well. What we are not happy about is the way you exceeded your brief by working your way into Morlands. Flying their prototypes, indeed! Cop-and-robber escapades up dark alleys! We have better things for you to do than that.'

'Tony,' I warned, 'you can talk like that all day and not convince me.'

'Convince you of what?'

'That you've not been got at.'

He chose to evade the challenge. 'If Morlands have sabotage on their hands,' he said, 'it's a case for the police. It's not what we pay you for.'

'You know perfectly well that Morlands can't go to the police. It would knock their board and their shares sideways.'

'That's their problem,' he repeated. 'Your detective work stops at bits and pieces. People are nothing to do with it.'

'I'm the best sort of detective they have in the circumstances, Tony.' I rose and made for the door.

'Where are you going?' he asked.

'You said you weren't expecting me yet,' I said. 'Just imagine I haven't arrived.'

I took a train up to town to avoid the parking problem, and made my way to the Ministry. I was two hours working my way up through successive layers of guardians but eventually, with the right combination of threat and pleading, I arrived in front of the Permanent Under Secretary. He gave me five minutes, and a look which said that he was fully briefed not only on the background but on my recent progress through his department. He heard me out and then stacked up his points in a neat, political way.

'Let me be frank with you,' he said. I was instantly on my guard. 'I was against sending anyone from AIB on the basis on which you went to Morlands. I can hardly help the fact that Sir William Morland has my Minister's ear, but I fought hard to send a full, official investigation team or nothing at all. We are not in business to unscramble Morlands' messes for them.'

I said nothing, wondering whether he was going to give me the kind of lead I needed.

'It was bad enough sending you in that unorthodox way. But when I discovered that your methods were becoming steadily more and more unorthodox, what would you expect me to do? I cannot acquiesce in a situation where a senior officer is kidnapped, for goodness' sake, and fails to inform the police!'

'Has Tony Morgan called you already, then?'

'Morgan? No.' For a moment, the Under Secretary was nonplussed. So was I; outside of Morlands, nobody but Tony was yet supposed to know about the kidnapping episode. I knew the man facing me would never tell me how he'd found out.

'I'm still in one piece, anyway. Whether I wanted the police was my business.'

'Not at all. It was Morlands' business. You have become too closely involved with Morlands, Mr Goddard. That is why your office was asked to move you to another assignment. Please don't deceive yourself I don't know why the police haven't been called in. Be that as it may, we are not to blame because the firm will not play by the book. It is something of an old habit of theirs.'

'A big firm like that is bound to have occasional conflicts of interest and opinion with the Ministry.' I was fishing, no more.

'Some of those conflicts, Goddard, have implications beyond the walls of *this* Ministry. And some of Morlands' methods have been questionable to say the least.'

'I'm afraid I don't understand.' My greediness to build on the half-lead he had fed me made me try too hard.

'Frankly, I should hope you don't.' He frowned and looked at his watch. 'I'm sorry, Goddard, that you should feel like this, but I am not going to have officers of your Department virtually seconded to Morlands or anywhere else as employees.'

'But suppose I can stop their second aircraft making a big hole in the middle of Barnsdale?'

He looked at me very hard. 'You would have to serve convincing proof of that.'

'That's the trouble. My proof is likely to take the form of a big hole.'

'That wouldn't be proof of your claim. It would simply show that Morlands had designed a rather, er, *unfortunate* aircraft.'

'I'm sure the inhabitants of the hole would thank you a lot for that,' I said, and left undismissed.

The tall figure swallowed his beer and I hastened to order him another. 'Reggie,' I said, 'I'm on an interesting one at the moment.'

'Morlands?'

'That's right. The whole thing is getting in rather a muddle; I'm so confused I don't know where to look first. Would you happen to know if anyone had been sniffing round the firm lately? The whole thing reeks of commercial secrecy, you see, and I'm wondering if a dreaded rival has stuck his oar in.'

Reggie lifted a shaggy eyebrow and studied me. He was a useful man to know, a security stalwart who had drifted into that line of business while still in the service. That was where I had first met him. Now he looked after the archives of the Board of Trade Intelligence Unit, an unlikely enough organisation but then everybody likes to get in on the act nowadays. Their function, nominally at least, was to check on the activities of British firms and act as a clearing-house for a wide range of industrial and economic stuff from overseas.

'I don't want to see their file or know what's in it,' I said encouragingly as he supped his pint. 'I just want to know if anyone has been taking a look at it lately.'

'It's been in and out like a bloody jack-in-the-box.' He leaned forward and wrinkled his nose. 'Actually, there's three files. One on Morland policy and personnel, one on their overseas selling activities—that's the hot one, I don't have to tell you that—and one on their relations with the Government as a whole.'

'That must be a honey as well.'

'Not really.' Reggie sounded disappointed. 'They keep it all on a very civilised level, you see. All smiles and underneath they hate each other's guts.'

'That's the way it has to be, you should hear them telling us to be nice to everybody. Look, has anyone taken a lot of interest in the personnel file lately? Somebody has set up a neat little organisation at Morlands and they couldn't have done it without a lot of dope on the key people. That's my starting point.'

He thought. He wasn't much to look at, but Reggie's mind was one of those waste-basket affairs, taking everything in without fear or favour and sorting it out later.

'Apart from my own blokes'—he included by inference everybody from his Minister downwards—'Defence are always nosing about. They mostly want to know who's trying to sell what overseas. Worried about the balance of power, and all that.' He dredged some more in the recesses of his memory. 'Come to think of it, Price-Thomas did have a go through the P1 file the other week.'

'That's the personnel file?'

'Yes. It struck me as slightly funny because they usually ask for the P2—the overseas relations one. You can see that.'

'How long did this guy have the P1 file?'

'Couple of days. Then he brought it back, and took the P3 instead.'

'Covering relations with the Aerospace Ministry?'

'And its many predecessors, yes.'

'How long did he have that one?'

'About the same time. He exchanged it for our S1 on the Aerospace Ministry.'

'Now you've lost me. What's an S1?'

'That's our run-down on all permanent Ministry staff. Have to know these things,' he said apologetically.

'You mean your Ministry keeps tabs on all the other Ministries?'

'Well, we all do, to some extent. Sometimes you have to know which way a particular cat is going to jump.'

'And if you see no harm in it, you share it out, right?
When Price-Thomas brought that one back, what did he
take next?'

'He didn't.' He held me suspended in silence for a moment.
'Young Burke came in.'

'Who's he?'

'Aerospace Ministry.'

'Why connect him with anyone from the Defence Ministry?'

'Because he and Price-Thomas are bosom buddies. Besides,' said Reggie, 'he asked for *all* the Morlands files—
no problem there—and his own S1, would you believe!' He
blinked indignantly over his beer. 'Can't be done. You don't
give a bloke your confidential assessment of him, do you?
He should have known that.'

'I suppose he should. What *can* you do?'

'Ask him who he's really interested in. Then you can
give him that bit of the file.'

'And which bit did he end up with?'

'AIB.'

'Now *that* I wouldn't like to see. Did you ask him why
he was making off with so much paper?'

'Report for his Minister,' said Reggie doubtfully.

'I wonder what that would have been about,' I said, and
ordered him another beer.

'Are you finally in this time?' Tony had simmered down.
It was a pity in a way, because I was going to get him all
stoked up again.

'Not for long.'

'I know it's not for long. You're going down to Penzance.'

'I'm going back to Yorkshire.'

He held himself in, and I had to admire his restraint.
'Suppose you explain,' he said. 'What have you been up to,
exactly?'

'I went to the Ministry and bullied my way into the
Presence.'

'Not the Minister!' He was genuinely aghast, in the way
that only a career civil servant can be.

'Not the Minister, the Permanent Under Secretary. Most enlightening, it was.'

'In what way?'

'He told me why I'd really been hauled down from Morlands. You could have saved me the trouble if you'd been honest about it. Somebody doesn't like what I've been doing up there, and it can only be because they want to see Morlands deeper yet in trouble.'

Tony looked as confused as only a man can who has been taken one stage beyond his comprehension.

'Somebody,' I ground on, 'doesn't like the things Morlands are selling to rich little countries spoiling for a fight. Perhaps it stops them sleeping at night. So they get on to Aerospace and tell them to stall on the Morlands crash investigation; and the Aerospace boys in their turn get all upset because I'm uncovering a nasty story. Their response is to order you to pull me out.'

'I hope you can confirm all that.'

'I could try, but it would compromise a friend of mine and anyway I've had enough of the devious workings of the official mind for one day. When the P.U.S. asks why I'm back in Yorkshire, tell him to ask his sidekick Burke who he's been talking to in the Ministry of Defence and whether he thinks it right to slant a briefing to favour a departmental vendetta at the expense of public safety.' I was so angry that my thinking stopped there, which was stupid. In fact it wasn't just stupid, it was damned nearly fatal.

# ◢ 14 ◣

'Darling,' I said to Liz, 'do you know our young Mr Burke at the Ministry?'

'I think he's rather dreamy.' She smiled archly.

'Known him long?'

I watched her frame a wicked answer and change her mind. 'You introduced us, Neil, at some party last year. Reception for some visiting fireman from America, it was.'

'Have you seen him since?'

'Once or twice. He moves in the right circles.' She had a gift for saying things like that without making them sound like lines from period-piece comedies. 'I think he has money of his own, he lives far too well to be existing on a Ministry salary.'

'I expect his daddy is something or other.'

'His daddy is at the Ministry of Defence. High, I believe.'

'Is he, now?' Another piece of the puzzle slid into place. 'Have you seen him recently?'

'Really, Neil!' She gave a nervous giggle of embarrassment. 'Why go on about him like this?'

'You wouldn't have seen him last week, for instance?'

'What if I did?' She tried to look angry to make up for the tacit admission.

'I just thought maybe he asked you to have a go at getting me down to London, away from here.'

'So he did! I thought it was very nice of him. Most men would have tried to take advantage, instead of telling a girl she ought to retrieve her husband.'

'That depends whether his mind is on higher things. Just tell me how it happened,' I sighed. 'What did he say?'

'He said the Morlands thing was coming to a grinding halt, that you were running your head into a brick wall looking for some reason for the crash because you couldn't accept it was John's fault.' She read the expression on my face. 'I'm only telling you what he *said*, Neil.'

'I know. Carry on.'

'He thought you shouldn't be allowed to waste your time and that you should never have been given the job in the first place, what with your personal interest in the thing. He said I should come up here and persuade you to report that you'd done your best and get you back to London.'

'And you believed him?'

'Why shouldn't I believe him? He wasn't out to gain anything, he was just trying to help. I was lonely,' she said, as though that explained everything. 'Oh, Neil, what did I do wrong?'

I remembered Jean's advice. 'Nothing, love,' I said gently. 'He used you, that's all, because he wanted me away from here. Because his daddy is high in the Ministry of Defence and they are worried sick about another fifty Morland Merlins going to fuel the fires of the Middle East.'

'I don't understand.'

'Good,' I said, but then I didn't understand either.

I told Jean about London and she didn't spot it either; at that stage we simply weren't equipped to sort it all out.

'Did Liz get in touch with you?' I asked. 'I told her to, but I don't know whether she took me seriously.'

'She wouldn't want anything to do with *me*, Neil.'

'On the contrary, she thinks you're rather nice, in a northern sort of way.'

'I'm flattered.' Jean grinned.

'Seriously, I'd like you to try and keep her well out of the way for a day or so if you can manage it. Show her the *Echo* office, and Barnsdale Park, and the high moors.'

'Why, Neil? Why do you want her out of the way?'

'Because I'm going to fly the second President with Arthur Morland.'

'That should be funny.' Jean reacted very calmly. 'Like as not you'll end up flying the two halves in different directions.'

'At least you can joke about it. Liz will have a fit if she ever knows, before or after. Can you keep her well clear of Morlands, do you think?'

'I don't know, Neil.' She looked thoughtful. 'You'll have to give me a day or two to try getting through to her. Maybe she'd like to come with me while I cover a few local stories. By our standards, she's almost a celebrity, you realise that?'

'I long ago stopped thinking of her like that. So should you.'

'There you go again, see?' Jean smiled her gentle smile. 'I'll see what I can do. With luck, we'll be miles away when you're flying the President.'

Thus it was that I carefully organised my biggest mistake of all.

In a way, the President was almost an anti-climax. I had spent so much time flying the simulator and the half-scale research model; concentrating absolutely, with no thought of the crash investigation that was still proceeding fruitlessly next door. Ominously, there had been no word from London. It looked as though I was on my own; I had no idea whether AIB was still paying my salary. By now the Ministry knew what I had done, and Tony would have had to relay my final outburst.

Arthur Morland and I had precious little room to spare in the tight flight deck. There, the seven-foot diameter of the main fuselage slimmed down to five, and there was just sufficient room between our seats to squeeze through and sit down. I recalled the ominous words of a Boscombe Down report on one aeroplane: 'Entry to the cockpit is extremely difficult. It should be made impossible.' But that wasn't how I felt about the President. Morland was scrupulously polite; I wondered what his father had said to him, or perhaps Arthur had enough sense to realise that whatever you think of a man, you have to establish a working relationship if he is sharing a first flight with you.

We both knew that if we ran into trouble it would be for real, for the President's design didn't run to ejector seats. Even if we made the fuselage door there was that great razor-blade of a wing waiting to sweep us up. This time there would be no technicians behind us looking after the recording gear, it would have to look after itself and if we came back in one piece we could take our pick of the volunteers from then on. But this flight was going to be ours alone, Arthur's and mine.

The view from the cockpit wasn't bad, despite the small screens, looming instrument panel and the radar housing ahead of us. The instrument layout was quite normal, another example of the design team's philosophy of keeping things cheap and easy to understand. We had all we needed, but no frills. If customers wanted frills once pro-

99

duction was under way, that would be fine; at a price, of course.

On Friday we made two long taxi runs on the big North Field runway, but on the second we pushed things slightly too far and cooked the brakes coming to a stop. By that time, though, the nose had been well up and we could feel her trying to go. They changed the brake units overnight and we taxied twice more on Saturday morning, but then the fuel pressure dropped on the port engine and by the time they had put it to rights it was too late. We were very much hampered by the shortness of the days, now that winter was coming on. Up in Barnsdale, it seemed to draw tangibly closer all the time.

'What do you think, Neil?' Morland looked across at me.

'Only an hour to sunset. But it's your aeroplane, you do what you like.'

'We'll be OK if we stick to the schedule.' He couldn't quite keep the excitement out of his voice, and I could hardly blame him. How would I have felt, had it been the first flight of an important aeroplane, and the key to the future of my father's firm? All the same, I liked my pilots past the excited stage. You stand more chance of making the right decisions that way.

'Go on, then. We'll try and keep something in hand.'

'Morland Tower, Alfa One, take-off this time.' Morland, as Chief Test Pilot, was Alfa One; I was Zulu One, so that everyone would know I was the odd man out.

'Roger Alfa One.' There was no emotion from the man in the tower, whatever he was feeling. Sunday or no, he would have most of the design team breathing down the back of his neck.

'Full power, then,' said Arthur.

I pushed the twin levers forward through the quadrant. Only the movement of needles betrayed the build-up of twenty tons of thrust.

'Reheat.'

Levers left through the gate and forward again. The extra ten tons of thrust were too much for the brakes, and we surged forward. I kept my hand on the throttle levers, tensed to chop the power if Morland changed his mind, one eye on the engine gauges and the other on the air-speed so that I could warn him when we were committed to take-off.

'Sixty.' A good sports car would have romped away from us up to this point, but now we were really accelerating. The President had a beautiful feeling of coming alive.

'Ninety.' There was still plenty of room to stop but time was running out fast. Morland's hands barely rested on the control column. The aircraft kept nicely straight without being asked.

'One-twenty. Rotate.' Two hundred feet a second, and Morland eased back on the column to lift the nosewheel, then moved it forward to hold the nose-up attitude. Five seconds and another thousand feet of runway, and there would be no stopping this side of the first flight.

'One forty-five, lift off.' Arthur came back on the column once more, and this time the whole aircraft lifted and everything went smooth and quiet. He checked forward again and we accelerated, the runway slowly sinking beneath us as the end approached. We had got the thing into the air, at any rate.

'Gear coming in,' I chanted. 'One-eighty; gear in and locked. Two-ten.' We were gathering speed at an ever-increasing rate, still climbing at a shallow angle. I wondered whether the very act of raising the undercarriage had set the switch that would finish us.

'Cancel reheat.' We were doing three hundred knots, and no longer needed the extra thrust. Morland trimmed into the climb, holding the speed where it was, and we went uphill at an indicated six thousand feet a minute.

'It looks as though we've done it.' He glanced across at me once more.

'We've done it all right. It's the next trick that bothers me.'

'Nonsense, man. Feel the way she flies; she's lovely.' He raised his hands from the wheel.

'I have control.' By now I had no doubt that Arthur was a natural, a very good pilot indeed; but he didn't go by the book. That was no reason why I should throw it overboard.

The President *was* lovely. My first impression was that the half-scale aircraft had given an extraordinarily good idea of how the full-size design would handle. There was the same crispness in roll, the same positive control and good damping in pitch. It felt much more like a fighter than a transport. The idea that anything could be basically wrong with the design made even less sense. I tried changing the power settings, and found only the small trim changes we had been expecting.

For almost an hour we followed the programme. We didn't go supersonic, or anything like it. Cautious engineers creep up on that sort of thing. The President would hit Mach 1, according to the programme, on her sixteenth flight; always assuming she made it past this one. Three hundred and fifty knots was the most we saw, and fifteen thousand feet was as high as we went. Most of the time we flew back and forth over eastern Yorkshire as the sun dipped down towards the broken stratus. Occasionally we spoke to Morland Tower, or to Northern Air Traffic headquarters.

We flew it down to ten knots above the calculated stall, flaps down and blowing on, wheels extended, and nothing happened that shouldn't have happened. But then nothing had happened to John when he had done the same thing.

'Morland Tower, Alfa One rejoining.' Arthur let them know in good time that we were coming back. Either he had visions of a welcoming committee, or I was doing him an injustice. The whole flight had a text-book quality about it and he had every reason to feel pleased, except for the final hurdle with which he was now faced. But then, he didn't see it like that; only I was alert for the hidden danger, convinced it was still there.

We went down through a cloud gap, found the base at four thousand feet and turned for Barnsdale. The landscape beneath turned from pleasant green to ravaged hinterland. Our speed came back until we were whispering along on a fraction of full power, and I put down the first ten degrees of flap as we picked up the beacon. The light was a good deal worse than when we had taken off, with the sun barely above the horizon, and invisible through the thickening stratus layer. Even so, the visibility was good enough for a routine approach. The runway lights were switched on to low intensity, a double row of brightness across the darkening countryside.

We curved over the line of the runway, just below the cloudbase, and straightened up for the downwind leg. I selected thirty degrees of flap as we slowed some more.

'Gear down.' Could Arthur Morland have shut the idea of impending disaster out of his mind? I checked the speed and moved the undercarriage lever. The three red lights appeared as the wheels moved, then changed to green as they locked down. No problem there, yet the sweat was beginning to form on my hands. We rolled smoothly to the left over Barnsdale itself, following the flight line of the first aircraft almost exactly, turning in a great sweep to bring us in line with the runway lights, still with four miles of final approach in which to sort everything out. It still looked like a textbook flight.

'Alfa One,' announced Morland, 'finals, three greens.'

'Roger Alfa One, clear land.' The controller's voice carried no hint of drama. I wondered how many people were down there on the balcony, who had come to see and who hadn't been able to bear the idea. Was there one amongst them who knew he would see a repeat performance? It was too late to think about that now, for we were committed.

The agreed approach procedure in the President was to fly the final turn at two hundred knots, then come back to one-seventy before putting down the rest of the flap, along with the flap blowing. I watched the speed fall, moved the flap lever and waited for the worst, but nothing happened.

Somehow, that only made things worse. There was nothing left to do, no more control movements to be made, nothing left to trigger off a disaster. Had I been wrong? Had John made a simple error, which I was too stubborn to accept? We were two miles short of the site of his crash, less than a minute away, and I could pick out the line of the railway. Everything looked fine, except for my nagging doubt. It was here, surely it was here ... the speed came slowly back, just as it should if we were to cross the runway threshold at a nice comfortable one-thirty knots.

'Just a shade slow, Arthur.' I was keyed up to a higher pitch than ever before, yet it arrived with such stealth that even I failed to see it. It seemed that Morland had allowed the speed to decay too fast, so that we were down to one-forty knots with a mile and a half still to go.

'Fifty per cent thrust, please.' He asked for a shade more power and I set it up, then looked back at the airspeed.

'Christ, Arthur, you're almost down to threshold speed!'

'Sorry.' He was perfectly calm. 'Must be more drag than we thought at approach speeds.'

At last my nagging doubt took charge, and I looked away from the airspeed indicator and across at Morland. 'How much forward movement do you have left?' I said quickly, for he was holding the column well forward between his knees.

'Not too much.' The helmet and mask made it impossible to read any expression on his face. 'Where's that power?'

I gave him another ten per cent thrust. 'Trim forward,' I said. 'Keep some movement in hand.' His thumb pushed the trim switch forward obediently and I watched carefully.

'Oh God,' he said suddenly, 'I can't hold her.' The nose was going up, and the speed still coming back. 'Full power!' he yelled. 'Full power!'

In that moment it hit me. Perhaps I was more at one with the way the aircraft felt, the more dispassionate observer; anyway, I hit my own trim switch, trimming back instead of forward. Since Arthur was still desperately thumbing his switch forward my effort merely stalled the trim motor, but even at that I felt the pitch rate decrease. The nose carried on rising, but not so fast. 'Trim back, quickly!' I snapped.

'Power!' Arthur practically screamed it this time, and his thumb still held the switch. The control column was right forward against the stops now. He reached across for the throttles, and as he did so I ducked across the front of him and chopped my hand down edgewise on his left thumb.

He yelped and let go the switch, but then I had to bring my elbow back sharply to keep him off the throttles. We were in trouble enough without pushing ourselves into it all the harder. The President was up at about forty-five degrees and the speed back to a hundred and twenty knots, almost at the stall. And if we stalled, British Rail would be out mending their line again.

Morland tried to seize his wheel once more, and I had no option but to swing a brutal fist in his direction, aiming at the junction of neck and shoulder. Any higher, and I would have done no more than break my knuckles on his helmet. He swayed sideways under the impact and I said, 'I have control,' as calmly as I was able, trying to get through to him. My own trim switch was still fully back.

He turned towards me again and I knew it was hopeless, there was nothing left in his eyes but unreasoning fear. Both hands stretched towards me and my own fist went between them and pushed the mask back into his face. It must have been painful, the upper edges of the mask cut into his lower eyelids and one of them split, and I could imagine the microphone grinding against his lips and teeth. He slumped backwards.

How long had I fought him? Nothing like as long as it felt, that was certain, but a good five seconds even so. I cast a panic-striken look at the panel, and found the air-speed indicator.

One hundred and thirty knots!

Now was the time for power. I eased the throttles open to full thrust. The President was still twenty degrees nose-up but the speed was moving in the right direction, taking us farther and farther from the stall. The runway slid past beneath us, a good two thousand feet below, and suddenly we were in cloud. We were gaining height as well as speed, and gaining it fast. Inside the cloud it was almost pitch black. I scanned the panel, trying to calm down and catch up mentally. All I wanted to do was set myself up straight and level, then establish a position.

A warning light flashed brightly, denying me the chance. I shoved out a rough hand to cancel it, then realised what it was trying to tell me; our speed was up through one-eighty knots, and too much for full flap. I raised the flap lever a notch and the next moment the control wheel moved smartly towards me. Even though I braced my arms it came through with enough force to leave me gasping. The President shuddered and the nose rose yet again, the speed falling off rapidly.

At that point I was on the verge of giving up. I was in danger of complete disorientation. Morland was moaning into his mask, doubled up in the left hand seat. The noise was strangled and nightmarish, and I realised his microphone had been damaged in the struggle. He was doubled up because his wheel had caught him a thump on its way back.

I let go the trim switch for the first time in something more than a minute, but it still took most of my strength to hold the column off the back stop. It was silly, the trimmer should long ago have reached the limit of its travel...

*That* was how they had done it!

At last I had a complete and rational explanation, and it did wonders for my morale. I trimmed forward normally and the load came off the column, until the President was easing up through the murk at two hundred knots and a thousand feet a minute. Although I knew how the trick was done, I needed some spare mental capacity to think of a way round it; and flying on instruments at low level would keep me too fully occupied. A minute later we broke through the cloud tops and I found to my surprise that the top edge of the setting sun was still visible.

'Alfa One, report please.' The controller's voice had been saying that for some time but I had been too busy to take any notice. With the coming of the light, and another three thousand feet beneath me, it had a chance to break through my concentration.

'Alfa One, six thousand and climbing, on one-eight-zero.'

'Roger Alfa One, what is your condition, please?' I tried to imagine what they must be thinking down there, having seen us climb crazily away from a beautiful approach and disappear into the cloud. And one man in particular would be thinking ...

106

'Alfa One, all intact, but we have a snag on the approach.'

'Roger Alfa One, we saw. Can you identify problem?'

If I gave them a run-down, the man responsible would stop at nothing to cover his tracks. Tactically the situation was very confused, and I had no time to work out the finer points of trying to fool the opposition. For the moment, I simply wanted to keep it all to myself, at least until I had landed. After that I would go to Morland and explain the whole thing.

'Yes, sir,' I said reassuringly to the controller. 'Part of it, at least,' I added cryptically.

'Do you wish technical advice, Alfa One? We have Mr Bates and most senior designers here.'

'Negative, I'll work it out up here. How are your local conditions now?'

'Less wind, Alfa One, zero-nine-zero at five knots. Cloud now eight octas at four thousand, we are on full runway and approach lighting.'

'Roger, Morland Tower. I have limited pitch control on final approach and may not be able to hold the target threshold speed. This next approach will be a full ILS on runway zero-seven.' It would be so dark down there that I would have to do a proper instrument approach; a fine prospect on top of everything else. I had half a mind to divert to Finningley or Binbrook, but if the President landed anywhere but at Barnsdale its secret would be out.

'Roger, Alfa One,' the controller was saying. 'Do you wish radar control to intersect the glide path?'

'Affirmative, sir. But I want to hold at ten to get my breath back.'

'How long, Alfa One?'

'Until I've got it back.' I was in no mood to argue with an inquisitive controller.

'Roger, Alfa One,' he said soothingly. 'Orbit at ten to establish radar identity. Northern ATC will be advised. What is your fuel state?'

Oh, God.

'Morland Tower, I have five thousand pounds only. Forget the hold, I'll take the approach from here.'

'Roger Alfa One, call Morland Radar on one-two-six-decimal-five.'

Clumsily, I set the frequency on the other VHF set. Five thousand pounds was six hundred gallons, which might sound a lot to the average car driver. But an overpowered medium-sized jet like the President uses the stuff slightly faster, especially at low level. Depending on how careful I was, I had sufficient for another half-hour at the outside, and half an hour can go very quickly when you are flying an instrument pattern.

The radar man came through and I turned on to his first course, throttled back and descending. I now knew that the trim reversed itself when the flaps were fully lowered and the blowing came on, but that didn't explain it all. Now we knew exactly where to look, their re-wiring, however cunning, would soon come to light. But why had we needed to trim in the first place? In the normal way we would have expected to ease forward on the column as the speed dropped, because of the natural tendency of the nose to rise. But we had run out of elevator travel altogether, as though the control surfaces had lost most of their effectiveness.

Could there have been a strong nose-up trim change? Nonsense. The wind tunnel tests would have shown it, and so would the half-scale aircraft. So the surfaces *had* lost their effectiveness, unless ... and then the rest of it fell into place.

In a way I had to admire the cunning of it, the way some devious mind had put it all together. What he had done was present me with two choices, both nasty. The first was to accept the present situation, fly the approach and hope I could keep the nose-up movement in hand by knowing about having to trim back instead of forward. But I couldn't be sure that would work, and there was no way to find out because I couldn't afford the fuel to go on messing about above cloud. Besides, I didn't think it would happen that high. Part of the scheme's misguided elegance was that it must be wired through an altitude switch. Otherwise, we would have found something—and so would John Rose—in the course of the preliminary handling investigation.

If it worked I might get down with little trouble, but if it didn't I would have to go round again and that would leave me very short of fuel. The alternative was to fly the approach with half flap and no blowing, putting the stalling speed up by forty knots or so and forcing me to come over the threshold at something like two hundred miles an hour—off an instrument approach, in an aeroplane making its first-ever landing.

The radar man had me coming round nicely, but I wanted to hurry things up, trying to make sure I had sufficient fuel for one more try. 'Morland Radar, can you get me on the beam close in?'

'How close, Alfa One?'

'Three miles to go?' The closer you hit the ILS beam, the less time you have to get yourself sorted out for the landing. Three miles was pretty close, especially at Barnsdale where there was plenty of higher ground and several obstructions near the field.

'Advise four miles and a thousand feet, Alfa One.'

'Roger, sir. Yes please.' I was aware that the radar man knew more about the airfield than I did. He turned me tighter, and I dropped back into the cloud. It was pitch black now, the sun had long since gone and the last feeble twilight was blotted out by the damp stratus. I wasn't even in practice for something like this, and concentrated like mad on the instruments.

There was a stir beside me and for the first time in ten minutes I remembered Arthur Morland. It was no time to administer first aid but I risked a glance and it was just in time, he was coming for me again. It was more difficult for both of us now, with the flight deck in darkness except for the faint green glow from the panels. He was a long way past thinking clearly, remembering only his previous panic and my brutal assault. His state did nothing for his aim or reflexes and I won, but only by shoving the mask back in his face once more. I felt slightly sick. Morland collapsed back in his seat, and I reached across and unfastened his mask to get the mess out of his mouth and give him some fresher air. The radar man was starting to sound anxious about my drifting off course. At least, I thought, he was spared any knowledge of what was really happening.

He brought me on to the beam exactly as he had promised, that man, but it was no time to thank him. I hoped I would still be around the next day, to do it then.

It is in the final stages of an instrument approach that a pilot endures his highest workload. He has to keep the crossed needles of the ILS dial in the centre, indicating that the aircraft is flying down the centre of the beam; he has to run through the final checklist, watch the speed and look for the runway all at once. Sure, I wasn't flying a complicated pattern in a busy control area and slotting between a dozen other flights like the airline boys, but they should have had my problems.

At four miles I was a thousand feet above the runway and that meant I should have been able to see the runway lights; but I couldn't. I remembered the tower telling me that the wind had dropped, and it seemed likely that Barnsdale had brewed up one of its famous fogs to add to my troubles. It was even less encouraging because I had elected to try the slow-speed, trimming-back approach to begin with, reserving the chance of going round again if the thing started to get out of hand, and doing a quick visual circuit for the high-speed landing. It was now clear that any sort of visual circuit was right out, at least for an aircraft of the President's performance.

I dared not leave the selection of flaps and blowing too late, for if I did I would have to shed speed very quickly just before touchdown, and at all costs I wanted things to happen as slowly as possible. At three miles I could see the glow of the lights in the haze but not their actual pattern. My speed was down to one-eighty knots and my thumb was ready on the trimmer. I put down the flaps, eased the wheel about half-way forward as the nose went up with the decrease in speed, then held any further rise with the trimmer.

I managed to keep it in check down to a hundred and thirty knots, piled on a little power to hold it at that and suddenly saw the runway lights sort themselves out into a pattern, with the approach lights rushing towards me. Cautiously I throttled back and trimmed some more, not wanting the speed to fall too soon. Half a mile from the threshold I was having to ease the wheel forward all the time to hold it. The lights were clear now, though the world held little else but blackness. A quarter of a mile; I used some more of my precious reserve of trim, rather than end up with the column against the forward stop. The approach lights were beneath me, the speed down to a hundred and twenty, and the President's nose was fifteen degrees above the horizontal, more or less where it should have been. Only two hundred yards remained to the green lights of the runway threshold.

Suddenly, the wheel would move no further forward. It was against the stop and I had already run out of trim, concentrating too hard on the runway and forgetting how little margin was in hand. I was so close I could have wept; for an instant I held it there, wondering about chopping everything and dumping her down. The green lights passed below, no more than fifty feet beneath me, only thirty feet from the wheels as they stretched down to meet the concrete. But it was no good; the nose was already up to twenty degrees, the speed down to a hundred and ten. If I chopped everything and hoped for the best she would either stall straight in, thumping her tail and breaking her back to carve a fiery trail down the runway, or she would gain enough height to spin in as her predecessor had done.

Thinking about the alternatives cost me a precious second or two. Even that was almost too long. The President was lolling about, all ready to stall, some fifty feet above the runway. It was no good; my clever approach, my knowledge of what the trouble really was had availed me nothing. I slammed open the throttles just in time, felt the nose rise even more in sympathy, then selected reheat and hoped the acceleration would get me out of trouble faster than the nose could point heavenwards.

It did, but not without making me sweat some more. The speed teetered for a moment around the stall, but with that much thrust underneath the President no longer weighed quite as much. I was conscious of crossing the downwind end of the runway, where the ground fell away from the banked-up threshold, and wondered how many

Sunday high teas I was spoiling. Relief flooded through me as I regained some margin of control and saw the speed and altitude increasing.

My relief didn't last long. The full-power overshoot was going through my slender fuel reserve like an orphanage outing through a cream tea. Not only that; I was in danger of losing the runway in the murk, and there was certainly no time to pull high and go through another instrument approach. With more than a hint of desperation I pulled round to the right in the climb, selected undercarriage up, cancelled reheat and raised the flaps. Just in time, I remembered to trim forward to neutral before bringing the flaps in; I didn't want the wheel whipping back at me as it had last time.

To begin with, it worked better than I might have hoped. As the speed built up I was able to throttle well back and establish a downwind heading, close in to the runway. Even so, my circuit would be a matter of intelligent guesswork; the airfield was no more than a fuzzy patch of brightness, hovering on the edge of the larger patch that was Barnsdale itself. A hundred and eighty knots; allow two miles for the length of the runway and a mile for the final approach—almost ludicrously short for the aircraft and the conditions, but with the fuel I had left it was the best chance I had. Three miles at a hundred and eighty was a nice convenient minute, but how far had I come already? I banged the stopwatch in a panic and watched the hand tick round, trying to estimate how long I had taken to work it out. My head was full of calculations clamouring for priority.

If I turned too early, I would cut my already slender chances of making a good approach almost to nothing. Too late, and I might not have the fuel for a last-chance climb and jump. On the whole, it would be better to have more room to play with than less. I forced myself to watch the second hand creep past thirty seconds. Instinct told me to turn; reason told me to hold out for another fifteen seconds. The fuel gauges were very much on the side of instinct, for I was operating within the range where their readings were almost a matter of chance with the last few hundred pounds or so sloshing around in the bottom of the tanks.

Forty seconds; I could stand it no longer, and started the final descending turn to the right. The bright smudge of Barnsdale spread in front of me and became brighter still, but it was impossible to tell where I was in relation to the edge of the town, the light was too diffuse for that. To join the glidepath a mile out I needed to be down below three hundred feet, and clear of the built-up area. I throttled back, selected half flap and undercarriage down once more, letting the speed fall off slightly to a hundred and seventy. The altimeter said five hundred feet, getting down to the sort of height where it could no longer be relied upon implicitly.

I tightened the turn and looked to the right, trying to pick out the approach lights from the flat, low-level glare. The visibility was diabolical. From the corner of my eye I saw the ILS flicker. I knew then that I must have crossed the glidepath at a fairly acute angle, already much too close in for comfort. Once more I slammed open the throttles and hauled the aircraft round; too late now to worry about the fuel state. She handled much better at the higher speed, that was one blessing, but in the next half-minute I would need all the margin she could give me.

The crossed ILS needles flickered again, only slightly more slowly, giving me no chance to check whether I was above or below the glidepath. I reversed the turn with a vicious swing of the wheel, heaving it towards me. The speed was too high, and the altimeter was trying to decide whether I was at a hundred and fifty or two hundred feet. At any moment I expected the dark mass of the Old Works to emerge in front of me. I tried to shut out the thought and anticipate my next intersection with the glidepath, checking the turn and coming back towards the runway heading before the needles flickered a third time.

It worked. The vertical needle came alive and I held it, banking through thirty degrees or more to make the capture. The horizontal needle stayed away up the top of the dial, confirming that I was too low. That was a considerable understatement. The altimeter, set to airfield height, had almost given up recording and one patch of brightness resolved itself into individual lights. There was a glow of sodium yellow on damp walls, almost close enough to touch. It was no time to remember that I was sitting twenty feet higher than the tail bumper. I eased back on the column to gain myself fifty feet and the horizontal needle whipped abruptly downwards across the dial. Almost at the same moment the next patch of brightness split into the centre-line and crossbars of the approach lighting.

To stop the aircraft ballooning above the glidepath, I pushed forward on the wheel, but too hard. I also needed to correct my heading. Things were happening too fast; I had plenty of control but I was paying the penalty for the flat, hot approach which the lack of flap blowing had forced on me. Violent manoeuvres at that height and speed could have only one conclusion unless I sorted things out very quickly.

I levelled the wings, cut the power and looked for the runway, too low now to worry about chasing the glide-path. The green line of the threshold lights came racing out to meet me with the first runway lights beyond, and their acute perspective angle told me how low I was. Too late to worry; at least the speed would mean a flatter approach and a more level attitude.

It might have been enough to enable me to get away with it, but in fact I had cut the margin just a shade too fine. The President shuddered as the port main under-carriage ripped through the final crossbar of the approach lights, and the wheel jumped in my hands. There was just time to haul back before we hit, a sort of token rounding-out to cushion the thump, but we bounced and sailed along, the runway lights flashing on either side.

My mind was still working in top gear, so that everything seemed to happen in slow motion. I had started working out how much runway remained when the second bounce came. The lights on my left were rather close, but I dared not bank to the right. The speed was too low, and I would risk sticking the starboard wingtip in the deck. The classic answer was to go round again, but I hardly had enough fuel to reach the end of the runway, let alone go along with what the book said. Instead I shoved the wheel forward and we touched the third time. This time we stayed on the ground, still travelling very fast.

There was a lurch towards the left hand lights and I realised that the port mainwheels had been damaged in their contact on the approach. The only thing I could do was apply right rudder and reverse thrust on the starboard engine only, leaving the wheelbrakes alone. Reluctantly the President straightened up, but the speed fell all too slowly and the runway lights continued to flick past one after the other.

In desperation I brought in reverse thrust on the port engine also, and we slowed up more quickly but veered to the left again. There was nothing I could do to hold it. The runway lights passed beneath me and the nosewheel collected one of them on the way, and then the aircraft shuddered as the wheels dug into the soft turf. The air was full of flying debris kicked up by the reverse thrust. A building loomed ahead and I chanced trying the brakes but nothing happened, the wheels were skidding already.

At least, I thought, it wouldn't be too bad. The speed was down to a fast running pace and I was strapped in. Then there was a thump which shook the whole aircraft as we ran on to a hard surface. The brakes bit at last and we swung round in a wild turn to the right. I cut the high-pressure cocks, starving the engines of fuel, and the thunder around me died. Suddenly things weren't happening so fast any more, and my mind slowed down to keep pace. The President rolled forward a few more yards and came to a stop.

There were lights, vehicles, people; apparent panic outside. It came to me as a shock that at no time during that last wild circuit had I said anything to the tower; I was still tuned to the radar frequency. I couldn't hear a thing. The drench of sweat made me shiver as reaction set in, and I dragged off my helmet and felt sick, leaning over the wheel. It was then that Arthur Morland hit me, though I didn't realise it until much later. All I saw was the sudden descent of blackness, and then nothing.

# ◢15◣

It was nice to wake up between clean sheets, with nothing to worry about. I lay for some time wondering whether there was anything I *ought* to be worrying about. Not really; I was very comfortable as I was and there didn't seem to be much point in dreaming up worries. People gave themselves ulcers that way. The room was pale and dimly lit. Where had I been, why was I in a place I didn't recognise? But that was a worry, and I was determined not to worry.

A door opened, admitting a flood of light and then, in the fullness of time, a face. It hurt my eyes to look up and try to recognise who I was, but even with the effort came the thought that I didn't know anybody, so it wouldn't matter.

'You're awake!'

It was as I thought. I didn't recognise her, nor did I see why she should sound so surprised at my waking. I wanted to nod but my head wouldn't move, so I settled for speaking only to discover that didn't work too well either. My efforts were rewarded with an uncivilised croak. Things were going badly with me.

'Relax,' she said. 'You've had a very nasty knock on the head. Don't try moving, you'll only hurt yourself.'

She was so patently right that I contented myself with rolling my eyes as far as they would go to pick up any extra information. Their focus improved with every second and I could control their movement well enough. They didn't seem to have me hooked up to any machine or set of tubing, that was something. I looked back at her and she resolved into a pretty face and a smart white uniform, so I tried to tell her I understood. Perhaps she divined as much from the second croak, for she nodded and retired, closing the door behind her, leaving me immobile.

The faces changed all the time, and time itself had no meaning. There was no way I could keep track of it. All the same I improved. It was a sort of game, regaining more and more control. When I tired of it, the patience of my starched visitors urged me on. Nothing made sense, but I wanted to please them. Why didn't I recognise anybody?

I recognised *him* at once, and it was almost too much. Everything that had been hiding just below the surface came out with a rush and overwhelmed me. Maybe that was sheer luck; anyway, it was more than I could take, and I passed out. The tall tweed figure with the piercing blue eyes regarded me aghast as I moaned and fell back. When I awoke, I was alone once more.

I had to start from square one, thinking quickly and logically, not knowing what line they would take and lacking one of my own. What would Arthur Morland have told them? I put myself in his position. The truth? Hardly. I would say there had been a fight in the aircraft; Goddard had gone mad and Morland had managed to overpower me and pull off a brilliant landing at the same time. Would they have believed that?

They might. That was largely my fault, for speaking so little to the ground. The voice tapes would tell them that Morland had flown the first approach, and I the second. There would be no indication who had flown the third. On the whole, I was still glad I had given the plotter-in-chief no idea that I had worked it all out, though it made my present position much more difficult.

I *had* worked it out. I knew exactly how the thing had been worked, but still had no idea who was behind it. For that I would need to start with the proof and find the lowest links in the chain, working my way up by degrees to the fountain-head.

But would they let me do that? The white uniforms, the

high standard of attention, the looming presence of old Morland himself, all pointed to one thing. They had me in a private nursing home. It fitted maddeningly well. No slur on the Morland name, no suggestion that the President was no good—or that Arthur Morland was no good, come to that. Was that why there had been no sign of Liz, still less of Jean?

I had attacked Arthur Morland, that was how they would see it. How would he have explained away the two missed approaches? Easy; I had gone mad during the first approach, taken over, gone round and tried for myself. Then the gallant Arthur would have struggled to regain control when I overshot, and brought the President home on a wing, a prayer and the last five hundred pounds of fuel. With nothing to gainsay him, that should set Arthur up as a hero, and convince them I was round the bend.

There was a nasty corollary to it all. I guessed from the state he had been in that Arthur would have no clear recollection of what had actually happened. He was quite capable of convincing himself of the truth of some such story, and that in turn meant that once the President had been repaired, he would fly it again. If they *all* believed him, they would miss the wiring changes and he would crash after all.

There was still the joker in the pack, the man who had organised the sabotage in the first place. He would have been worried stiff at my having landed the President in one piece. His obvious course of action was to go along with Arthur's story, try to keep me out of circulation and encourage the flight test team to press on with the programme, now running even further behind schedule.

Whose idea had it been, to whisk me off to some private clinic? Possibly, though not definitely, the man I was after. Would he be content to see me kept here, or would he want to make absolutely sure? The place wasn't too far from Barnsdale, I judged, or old Morland wouldn't have turned up to glare at me. That had been a stroke of luck, throwing the picture into focus, yet allowing me time to think before anything else happened. I had certainly been suffering from amnesia: perhaps it was best that I should continue to do so. For the time being at least. I lay back and worried.

His smile was as well organised as ever. He breezed in and sat himself down, and his eyes never left me; but that could have been sheer force of habit.

'So he decided to send you, did he?' My growl saved him having to cast round for an opening. He should have been grateful instead of wiping the smile off his face.

'How do you mean, old chap?' A neutral, careful probe.

'Old Morland. I went all funny and passed out on him, didn't I? So much came back with a rush, that was the trouble.'

'Came back, did it?' Simpson combined the anxious visitor and dutiful company servant to perfection.

'Hell, no ... *he* came back. Morlands came back, and the President...' I watched his face, but there was nothing beyond an inviting rise of the eyebrows. If George Simpson was worried, he wasn't letting it show. 'I've been trying to worry out the rest,' I said with well-rehearsed dishonesty, 'but I come up against a sort of blank wall. Did we fly the President? Is that how I landed up in here?' I had worked out not just the words but the intonation of the whole thing. My main worry was whether it would sound wooden and scripted.

'You flew it all right.' He confessed that much, then switched subjects. 'What do you mean, when you say Sir William *sent* me?'

'Of course he sent you. He wants to find out how I am, he wants me summed up. Am I thinking straight? I don't remember what happened, George, so how should I think?'

'You remember nothing whatever of the flight?' I searched for hope or fear in his voice, but there was only care.

'When so much came back, I thought the rest would follow. But it didn't, and now I don't think it will. What happened, George? You said we flew it. Is it damaged? Did anything happen to Arthur Morland?'

'He's in a better state than you are, though he was in something of a mess afterwards.' Simpson knew the value of sticking close to the truth where it would do no harm.

'Around the face,' he went on, and paused. I slid my puzzled expression into place.

'We crunched it? How did we get out?'

'You landed fairly heavily,' he said. 'You seemed to be having some trouble on the approach.' It was encouraging that he was slanting his questions—and his probings—as though he accepted my amnesia and wanted to see if my memory was capable of revival. 'The President is still in one piece,' he said. 'There is some undercarriage damage, no more. She'll fly again soon.'

I was in an awkward situation because George, like everyone except the saboteur, would believe Arthur's story. It was the only one he could reasonably tell, other than the truth. For a moment I tried to work out the consequences of Arthur telling the truth, but it was too much. Had he done so, the extent of my knowledge would have been plain and they would have had Bates and Old grilling me the moment I came round, instead of Simpson feeling his way round my position. George had undoubtedly been charged with making sure I could remember nothing of the flight. That way they could keep the story in a tight little circle and nobody need ever know. But what would Arthur Morland say if we ever came face to face? The others would be able to control themselves, but ... then I realised that I stood little chance of meeting Arthur again unless I could stop him flying the President in its present state.

'What day is it?' I said suddenly.

'Tuesday.' Simpson looked wary.

'*Which* Tuesday, George? How long have I been here?'

'Since last Sunday.'

'Nine days!' I lapsed into thought. They must be well on the way to having the President airworthy again. I had kept no track of time at first. Somehow it had seemed like months, my sheer emptiness of mind had seen to that. 'Who pays for me, here?' I asked. 'Morlands, or the Ministry?'

'Morlands, of course. You don't really want the Ministry to know how you came to be in this state, do you?'

He had a point there. The Ministry had reacted badly enough to everything I had done previously. If they now discovered I had been involved in a first flight, let alone an accident to a first flight, it would turn hair grey over a considerable area of Whitehall. Even so, I had the impression that my mention of the Ministry had worried George slightly.

'Have they not asked after me?' It was the only handle I had to shift him, otherwise I would still be in medical hands after Christmas. If gentle pressure didn't do it, I could always develop an obsession; it might even reassure them.

'The Ministry understands that you're very ill.'

'I'm not *that* ill.'

'Amnesia? What else have you forgotten? Wouldn't you prefer to take the sick leave and try remembering the rest?'

'They won't stand for that.' They wouldn't, either; at least, not indefinitely. 'Have they sent anyone to see me?'

'Yes.' He was ready for that one. 'It was very early on; you were still unconscious.'

'And what did you say had happened?'

'Car crash.' I regret the dishonesty, his smile seemed to say, but we thought you would prefer it that way.

'And they didn't have time to stay. What about my wife?' I had been storing that one up to throw at him but it failed to make any visible impression.

'She went back to London.' His studied lack of expression was almost an expression in itself. 'She was very upset. Apparently she drew the obvious conclusion from the President's flight and your injuries. I gather she doesn't like you test flying.'

'Dear Liz, so faithful.'

'Don't be like that, Goddard. You were the one who tried to keep it from her.'

'That's right. What about Miss Partington?'

'Who?' He frowned. So did I, mentally; a top-flight security officer like George ought not to profess ignorance of the staff of the local press. Especially after referring to my attempt to keep Liz clear of my flying.

'Jean Partington,' I offered. 'Bert's daughter; you know, the Superintendent in Number Five. She's a reporter on the *Barnsdale Echo*.'

'My dear chap,' he shook his head, 'I think we ought to

keep you clear of reporters for a bit.' He looked at his watch.

'Aren't I a lucky chap, George?' I said. He looked at me, brow furrowed. He mustn't think I was longing for Jean, though I was; she was almost the only person I could trust enough to talk to, who might help me straighten out my ideas. It was borne in upon me that I didn't trust George, but then I didn't trust anyone.

'Lucky?' he said.

'Flat on my back; employers don't care, wife has run off, and I don't even know what happened.'

'Don't *worry*, old chap.' He was positively fatherly. It had been my punch line, complete with authentic note of despair. 'We *do* care,' he went on. 'The Ministry cares. We want you to get well as soon as you can.'

'Thank you, George, you're a real comfort to me.'

He replaced his standard smile and left.

I would have trusted Morland, Old Morland that was, but he wouldn't have trusted me, not after I had half-killed his only son and nearly written off his latest aircraft into the bargain. And there was nobody else in Morlands' inner councils that I could trust, because any one of them might turn out to have been just the wrong man to confide in. If that happened, and he knew I was working out a way to pin him down, I might find myself very permanently pre-empted. That sounded highly melodramatic, but he was going to kill Arthur Morland, was he not, by standing back and letting him fly the President again? Paradoxically, the only one in the clear was Lovegrove, and *he* wouldn't touch me with a bargepole.

I would have to control myself, to think straight, even here on my own with no light to steer by. The worst thing of all was not knowing how much time I had left. The sheer frustration of having the lead, of knowing how to salvage the President programme and find out who had tried to wreck it, yet being cut off from any means of doing it...

I began to identify my objectives and sort them into an order of priority.

\*　　\*　　\*

'George, I want to see someone from the Ministry.' It was now Wednesday; henceforth I could keep track, even if it meant scratching marks on the wall behind the bed.

'Of course, old chap.' He hardly bothered to hide his patronising tone. 'And what will you tell them that they don't know already?'

'I don't know.' Not much, I didn't, but he left me no alternative to the clumsy dodge while I thought hard. 'They ought to know how I am, that I want to get back to work.'

'They take that for granted.' He smiled. 'But they don't want you rushing things until you're really fit.'

'I am fit, George.' I interlocked my fingers and pushed them away. He didn't seem impressed.

'You're only fit when the staff here say so,' he warned.

That did it. I had to push him harder, now he had given me the opening. I was fed up with his easy retrieval of every ball I sent into his court.

'No, George.'

He looked startled. 'I'm sorry?'

'I said no. Morland pays the bill. Are you sure *they* don't decide when I'm fit enough?'

'What do you mean by that?' He knew very well, but he hadn't been prepared for a frontal assault.

'Who wants to keep me here, George? What are they scared I'll say? How long before it's safe to let me out, George? Does something have to happen first, like the next flight of the President?'

'Don't go paranoid on us, Goddard.' Simpson was back on balance, with an effort. I wondered whether the interview was being recorded. In a place like that, they might do anything.

'I'm sorry, George.' There was no alternative to backing down a bit. 'It's just being cooped up here, seeing nobody. One gets to thinking, to adding two and two. Sorry if I made it five.'

'You think too hard, that's your trouble.' George was doing some thinking on his own behalf, that much was plain.

'Maybe.' I hesitated before taking the plunge. 'But we can't let this thing drag on too long. It's not just the

Ministry. I made one or two inquiries on my own account when I was down in London, sniffing around the sabotage side of the first crash.' I was picking my way through a verbal minefield and he waited patiently for me to reach the middle. 'I mean, one or two people are going to start wondering if I don't show up.'

'You make it sound as though you'd been kidnapped, or something.' He didn't sound in the least amused.

'Well, look at it from my point of view; or theirs. We don't want them trampling all over the place, do we? That's the trouble, one or two of my friends have nothing to do but exercise their connections.' It wasn't a very graceful threat, or a very real one, except that I *did* know a few such characters.

No wonder George was thinking. He would be weighing the risk of somebody tumbling to his fake car crash against the risk of my recovering the memories he thought I'd lost. If I remembered anything of that last flight and told the Ministry, the story could be used as a political weapon of the first order—even when told Arthur Morland's way. If I couldn't remember, they would do better to send me packing: except that anything might act as a catalyst to fill my memory gaps. That was how George would see it. His problem, careful, patient man that he was, stemmed from any doubt he might have that I did remember, or *would* remember.

'Let me talk to the medical director,' he said.

They let me out the next day. It was nicely done. They took some X-rays and showed me how the bump on my head had gone down, though they didn't explain how a bump had appeared on the back of my head in the first place, and I didn't feel like pushing my luck. They gave me a better check-over than I had endured for any flying medical and pronounced me fit, within limits. Looking over their shoulders at some of the values—to say nothing of how I felt—I was less sure. I had been on my back for too long.

George Simpson's attitude was that of a man who had worked the oracle. He beamed his way in, took charge of me, thanked everyone and ushered me out. Twenty minutes later, one of my theories was confirmed, for we arrived at the airfield.

'Why here?' I asked. It made no sense to me. I had been expecting Simpson to shove me on a train for London, not bring me back to the very place where my memory was most likely to fill in the gaps from which he supposed it to be suffering.

'Why not here?' He waved to the gateman. Now that I was inside the perimeter, I thought, how easy would it be to get out again? I could try the telephone, but it was so easy to monitor calls from a closed area like Morlands. 'We thought it would reassure you to see the President,' said George, even more unexpectedly. 'You can see how far we've progressed with the crash investigation, too, though we're more or less bogged down according to Brian Bates.'

Bates might be bogged down, but I wasn't. On impulse I said, 'Could I see the film of our landing?'

Simpson's look was almost grateful. 'It was dark when you landed, after all that trouble. Do you really not remember?'

'I'm sorry,' I said, 'but I don't. Perhaps the President will remind me.'

'Yes,' he nodded. 'Perhaps it will.'

And if he thought it had, what then? It made no difference whether George was the company's man or the saboteur, his reaction would be the same in principle. He would not easily let me go.

I kept him happy enough. No matter how hard he looked for a sign, nothing showed, I was sure, except the vagueness in which I had schooled myself. The limits of the knowledge to which I would admit were clearly staked out in my mind. We strolled round the President and looked with interest at the work that had been done on the undercarriage. Several of the shop-floor people looked at me strangely. How much did they know? Had some of them been on hand to find us in the cockpit, and had they jumped to their own conclusions? If they had, it would certainly surprise them to see me wandering around: a point in favour of bringing me back.

I sat in the aircraft's right hand seat and shook my head. George looked suitably sorry, though underneath it all I would have taken long odds that he felt a great deal happier. 'How is Arthur Morland?' I asked, fingering the control wheel.

'Recovering nicely. Taking a few days' rest, on doctor's orders. You should be doing the same. We'll pack you off into the sunshine this evening.' He smiled some more.

'We thought,' he said, 'that you'd like to see our final report on the crash, and a summary of your flight results. You may like to chew it over, and grind out something to keep your people happy. We kept the same office for you.'

Really, he was too kind, feeding out the rope in the hope that I would hang myself after all.

Even so, it was awkward. He had presented me with a golden chance to pick up the proof I needed, but did I dare take advantage of it? I spent a quarter of an hour going over the office for microphones before I realised how twitchy and off-balance I was getting; a microphone would be no good to them unless I started talking to myself. The telephone was out; that wasn't worth the risk. It took another spell of close thinking to convince me that I could pass off my search for proof as a simple cross-checking of their own crash findings.

That drove me to settle down with their report and read it through quickly and thoroughly, wondering what kind of cover-up job they were running. It wasn't much of a job, in the event; they spent a hundred pages coming to the conclusion that they didn't know what had caused John's crash. Their guess, on the popular *reductio ad absurdum* basis, was that he had been the victim of some kind of seizure at a critical stage in the approach, too late for his co-pilot to do anything about it. The approach phase, they said, was known to be tricky, for the second aircraft had run into trouble at the same stage. They had amended the story I credited to Morland—there was no mention of me at all—and I glanced through the concluding paragraphs about control circuit modifications to increase the damping in pitch at low airspeeds.

Why did they not mention me? Because I couldn't remember, could throw no light on the matter, that's what they would say. Besides, they were keeping me out of trouble with the Ministry, weren't they? And if I *could* remember, they might as well throw their report out of the window. They must have been breathing easier at that moment, and I hadn't the heart to disillusion them.

I sat and doodled angrily, using paper as a substitute for a friendly ear. It was plain enough from the report, and the general attitude, that most people either believed Morland's story or lacked any clue as to what had happened. Only a select few would have been admitted to the secret. No wonder they were handling me with kid gloves, while keeping Arthur well out of harm's way.

More and more, it appeared that only two people knew the whole truth; me, and the man who had set the plot up in the first place. What was he thinking, my opponent? The chances of *his* having accepted Arthur's story were small. He would be lined up with the rest of Morlands hoping my memory had truly failed.

Unwittingly, Arthur Morland had cut me off. Nobody at Morlands wanted anything to do with me, and my own office would have the hatchet good and sharp. There would be little chance of help from that quarter. There remained some of my better-connected friends, though I stood to gain little by passing the buck to them, and the civil police, who wouldn't be interested unless I presented them with evidence of crime committed.

That brought my thinking back full circle. I was still the investigating inspector, I would have to rummage around and find the evidence. My starting point would be the drawing store in Number Five building, where the whole President was stored, on paper, beside the shop where the aircraft was being built. I went across and withdrew several electrical system drawings, stowed them away in my office, and then called Brian Bates.

The main drawing office was one of those vast open-plan rooms where you can hardly see from one end to the other for drawing-boards and cigarette smoke. The air con-

ditioning was fighting a losing battle with the winter afternoon fug. Even Bates' position warranted no more than a
glass-walled sub-division of an office, overlooking the whole
joyful scene.

'Have you really given up?' I said, waving the report at
him.

He looked at me sharply. I guessed he was privy to Morland's story, and knew of my supposed loss of memory.
Either that, or he was the man I was after, there was no
way to tell without evidence.

'We've been through it time and time again,' he said. He
looked even older than the last time I had seen him. 'John
Rose's flight,' he went on, 'your flight, back to the wind
tunnel and the computer; nothing. Heavens, Goddard,' he
burst out, 'Arthur Morland comes back with some tale
about it being almost uncontrollable in pitch at low speed,
and *you* don't remember a thing! What would you do in
my position?'

I was on the verge of telling him, but the seeds of doubt
were sown deep in my mind. I contented myself by murmur-
ing, 'It depends what your position really is.'

'I beg your pardon?' He sounded genuinely puzzled. If
he were the one I was seeking, his acting matched his engineering ability, but even that was not impossible.

'Just thinking. Sorry.' I glanced out of the door. 'You'll
fly the second aircraft again soon?'

'Young Arthur's waiting for the off. You've seen the
modifications we're putting in?' He nodded towards my
copy of the report.

'I've seen them.'

'Load of rubbish,' he growled. 'There's something more
wrong with it than that. It's like trying to cure pneumonia
with aspirin.'

'But you'll let it fly anyway?'

'Damn them all, there's nothing *wrong* with the thing! I
need proof, Goddard, proof ... if I could point to something and say look, this is all wrong, we'll have to tear her
apart and start again, fair enough. But everything says
she ought to fly and the word is she's going to.'

'Who's pushing for it, Brian?'

'What do you mean?'

'Who's taking the line that you should bury your fears and get on with the third flight?'

'Arthur Morland, like I said.' He looked at me narrowly, not liking my approach. It was, if anything, too rational.

'Nobody else?' I pressed him.

'Jack Old, I suppose.' Bates paused painfully. 'He says the sooner we fly it or crash it, the better.'

'That's not a very responsible line for your flight test chief to take.'

'He doesn't mean it that way, of course.' He pursed his lips like a cornered schoolboy trying not to sneak. 'He's fed up with the deal, we all are. Don't talk about responsibility, we've said our piece and been overruled. She'll fly again, with the modifications.'

'Have you changed the ground test schedule at all?'

'Man, we've practically doubled it. She checks out like a dream.'

'Nevertheless, you're convinced we've missed something.'

'That's still my opinion, but it doesn't carry sufficient weight with the directors.' No Chief Designer of Morlands had ever been on the board; it was another of the company's unique policies that he should concentrate entirely on engineering. 'Dredge that memory of yours, Goddard,' pleaded Bates. 'Are you sure the answer isn't locked in there somewhere?'

'Locked is the operative word. That's assuming there is an answer.' I wanted to leave it at that. 'Look, Brian, can I try a little theory of mine, just to keep me occupied until I go home?'

'Be my guest.'

'I want to look at some of the electrical systems drawings.'

'But you have them all, over in Number Five.'

'Yes,' I said cautiously, 'but they're using them all the time over there. Could I see the file originals in your electrical drawing section?'

Bates frowned. 'Which ones?'

'Quite a few.' The last thing I wanted to do was be specific. If Brian Bates was the man I wanted, it might be suicidal to tell him which circuits really interested me. He looked as though he expected me to carry on, but I didn't. The awkward silence stretched unwillingly through the next few seconds, and then he nodded.

Adam Szydlowski was more British than the British. Morland's resident electrical genius, a scruffy figure dedicated to raising his own smoke screen with the biggest pipe in the place.

'Call me Adam.' He waved the pipe at a spare stool. 'I can't bear to hear good Polish spoken bad.'

I was relieved, and said so.

'Never mind. You want drawings, I hear. Why so? You think we make mistakes over here?'

'Not at all.' It was such a drawback having to tread so carefully whoever I was dealing with. 'All I was thinking was that maybe a little mistake crept in, somewhere between the drawing board and the assembly line.'

'Not possible. Look,' said Adam, shifting round on his stool so that he faced me squarely, 'we draw drawings, yes? Every man is good, but every drawing is checked all the same. Mostly by me.' He puffed a challenging stream of smoke towards the roof space. 'Then it goes to tracing. All good girls, the tracers, but the tracing comes back here for checking anyway. Then the tracing goes to the print shop, and how can the printers change a tracing? And finally the prints are issued to the shops. Mind you,' he said, jumping in with a jab of stubby finger before I could say a word, 'the boys in the hangars, they do a job, it's checked. Nobody ever carries a can single-handed in this place, see?'

'Except you, Adam.'

'Oh yes, except poor Adam. But with me the check is easy; the thing must work, or it isn't right.'

'But the President didn't work.'

'Ah! The electrics, *they* work. Brian Bates told you about the ground test schedule? Every circuit, Mr Goddard, every circuit works how it should. You want to find out what's wrong with the President, you look somewhere else.'

'Where else, Adam?'

'Anywhere else. You think some little wire coming adrift would crash the thing? You're crazy.' He stumped off to find the drawings, and I spent the next half-hour making notes. Every so often, I looked up to see who was watching.

It is one thing to guess how something must have been done, yet another to find confirmation. It took only a few minutes to find what I was looking for, and then I had them. The sheer simplicity of the thing was overwhelming. I sketched a few circuits to make sure I was right.

Armed with these, I retreated to the shop floor in Number Five for another look at the wreckage of the first aircraft. I was certain in my own mind as to what I would find, but I had to see with my own eyes the evidence of malice aforethought.

Bert Partington came to meet me. 'Nice to see you about again, Mr Goddard.'

'It's nice still to be in one piece, Bert.' I watched for the half-hidden reaction, but there was nothing behind his grin.

'What would you be looking for now, Mr Goddard?'

'Bits and pieces, Bert.' I fenced him off like all the others. My mistrust was becoming an obsession.

'Go ahead, then.' He made no move to come with me, to watch what I would do.

'Thanks,' I acknowledged, and then on impulse: 'How's Jean?'

'Fine, as far as I know. I thought you might have been able to tell me.'

'Come again?'

'She went away with Mrs Goddard. Did nobody tell you? Perhaps they didn't know...' He sounded slightly embarrassed. 'We had a letter from Jean, yesterday it would have been, from Spain.'

'Spain? Where in Spain? What are they doing there?'

'Jean said Mrs Goddard had taken your crash very badly ... that she needed looking after. I gather you've friends on the Costa Brava.' He avoided any hint of censure.

To be sure, we—or rather, Liz—knew some people at S'Agaro, and it would be entirely in character for her to beat a hasty retreat in some such direction. Two things worried me: Jean had been keeping Liz clear while I flew, and if the Ministry could accept a car crash story, why couldn't she? Apart from that, it was totally out of character for Jean to chuck up her job and rush off to Spain to look after the likes of Liz. There were plenty of others with more time and inclination for that sort of thing. It was even less like Jean to have left no message.

I poked around in the wreckage with half my mind elsewhere. It was sufficient to confirm that the microswitch wiring tallied with the drawings from the store; I had my proof. Somehow, it didn't matter so much any more.

George Simpson saw me on to the evening train for London.

'A holiday, old boy,' he said. 'Go to Spain, sit by a pool and wait for it all to come back. Give us a call if it does.'

'Spain?' I reacted more sharply than I should have done.

'Yes,' said George easily, 'Spain.' He fished inside his coat and produced an envelope. 'There might even be somebody to meet you.'

'I see.' I hoisted my case aboard and shook hands with him. It would have been nicer flying down, but even I knew it would be silly to risk it so soon after a hefty thump on the head. I fumed inwardly but he stayed on the platform until the whistle blew, the perfect host and perfect company servant, seeing a load of trouble out of his parish. The last I saw of him, as the train pulled out, he was still waving. With the sight of his diminishing figure came the thought that I should perhaps have trusted him after all. Now I would have to find some other way of stopping Arthur Morland killing himself and taking Morland Aircraft with him.

I opened his envelope. Inside was a BEA ticket for next morning's flight to Barcelona, ten thousand pesetas, and a compliments slip. 'If anything comes back,' George had scribbled, 'let *me* know.'

The first stop was Sheffield. It was farther than I wanted

to go, and to that extent a waste of time, but it gave me a chance to press on with my thinking. Picking the joker out of Morlands' pack would be far from easy, and it was still up to me to do the picking. If the police tried, they would like as not stampede the men they were after right underground.

Special Branch? I was not without contacts in that area, but strictly speaking they wouldn't be interested unless there was a security side to the whole thing. Indeed, if my reading of the basic motive was correct, the affair had its origins in security. I might be making even more trouble if I stirred things up from that direction.

The main thing was to stop the President flying again until it had been sorted out. The only man who could do that was Sir William Morland, and my chances of getting to see him were utterly remote. The screen would be round him by now; a screen of his own making, but reinforced with determination by the very man I wanted.

The train was running into the dim lights of Sheffield before I realised that, for the sake of a very small chance, there was another way. I trusted Jean, didn't I? In that case, I could surely trust her father too. After all, he worked in Number Five, not in the drawing office where the trick had been worked.

It was good reasoning, but I hadn't taken everything into account.

# ◢16◣

It was raining in Sheffield, an ill-named warm front was pushing north-eastwards over Yorkshire. It had done nothing to improve the temper of a ticket inspector who couldn't see why I was getting off in Sheffield when my ticket entitled me to go to London, and looking around the city I could appreciate his doubt. It took me ten minutes to find the bus station and another twenty to establish that I could return to Barnsdale by bus, changing only once and spending no more than an hour and a half on the journey. It was better than walking, but only just.

The *Barnsdale Echo* was running full pelt at ten o'clock. After the darkness and the steady drizzle outside, its front office seemed a cheerful place. The bustle of machinery, churning out the life of Barnsdale for tomorrow's consumption, filled the entire building. I had to half-shout to introduce myself.

'Jean Partington?' The Editor's office was quieter, but only just. The Editor himself was younger than I would have imagined, struggling to make the change from working journalist to administrator. 'Not a sign of her,' he said. 'Inconsiderate, really, and we're short-handed as it is.'

'But she would have known that.'

'Of course she did.'

I told him about the letter to Bert. 'Is it like her, to do a thing like that?' I asked. 'Rush off without telling you, I mean, assuming she'd go at all?'

'Most unlike. You know her, don't you? I mean,' he added hastily, 'she told us there might be a fresh story coming up on the Morlands crash, and I told her to stay with it. Was there really something to it?'

'There's a hell of a lot to it,' I said grimly, 'and more and more by the moment.'

The thought came to me that I wanted to look at Jean's flat. At least I would be able to see whether she had taken anything away with her, and she might have left some sign. Apart from that, however silly it sounds, I wanted to get as close to her as I could, to somehow establish enough contact to make my next job easier. Because my next job was to persuade Bert Partington to re-wire the President.

I need not have worried myself composing an introduction to the landlady, for Jean's flat was open and a light was on. The door gave to my push, and I stepped through into the tiny hallway, not daring to call. Was she home after all? Had she seen Liz safely installed and then come rushing back?

The light came from the sitting room on my left, so I shoved the door open gently. It swung wide to reveal a well-known figure lounging comfortably in the old armchair.

'Come in, Goddard,' he said amiably. 'I was more or less expecting you.'

'Hello, George. Still making sure I leave town?' I tried to sound calm, with decreasing success. There was a movement behind me. Getting out would pose more problems than gaining entry.

'Leave town? We wouldn't hear of you leaving town.' He smiled once more. 'We want you to stay for a few days. Why not sit down and have a drink?'

I took the seat, but not the drink. I needed every wit I could muster. 'A few days until the President flies again?'

'Exactly, old boy.'

Up to that point, I had just a slender hope that he might be looking after Morlands' interests, but George had now established his interest beyond all doubt. 'Why play it this way?' I asked. 'There was no way I could have pinned you down.'

'Oh, please don't think of me as pinned down, Goddard. Think on, as they say hereabouts; if I am here, where is the delightful Miss Partington? And where, come to that, is your wife? It was helpful of you to bring them together. My manpower is limited, and it helped quite a lot.'

'When did you get them?'

'Immediately after you had landed the President; much to my surprise, I must confess. My debt to Arthur Morland for rendering you harmless is considerable.'

'You've picked a nice way to repay it.'

'I'm surprised *you* should feel sorry for him.' George was relaxed, his coup completed. 'I never really swallowed your selective amnesia, Goddard. The people at the clinic were much too surprised for me to trust you. Still, you put on a good act, until you gave the game away this afternoon.'

'How did I do that?'

'Charging about all over the place, asking after electrical drawings in the main office, checking with copies from the Number Five store, looking at the switches in the wreckage...'

'All watched by Uncle George?'

'Indirectly, yes. You worried one of Adam's lads a good deal, he thought you were getting much too close. I have an obligation to my employees, you see.'

'Employees?'

'Stop being so carefully stupid, Goddard, it's too late. You know full well I didn't dream up the whole thing myself. I'm no engineer; I needed someone to produce a scheme that would work, once the idea had been put to him.'

'How did you do that? Blackmail, or just plain money?'

'That would be giving the game away.'

'Why, what have you got to lose now?' I sounded as bitter as I felt. 'Of course, you're the security officer, you're in a good position to get the people you need, one way or the other.' A thought came to me. 'How did they get at you, George?'

'It depends how you look at it, Goddard. A little squeeze, a lot of money, the temptation of something exciting.'

'George, we're talking about murder.'

'Nonsense.' His relaxation remained. I heard one of his people shift behind me. 'The aircraft fails to fly, that's all. No bomb, no sawing through wires, nothing to give the game away.'

'Nothing, George? Only me.'

'You're not *evidence*, Goddard. You can bleat in the wilderness, but you'll never prove anything. Even you would never have realised without flying the second aircraft, and you can take it from me that after this week nobody will ever put the President in his log book again.'

'So why bother with all this nonsense? Why grab the three of us?' He was beginning to annoy me.

'Spare me, Goddard. Why did you come back to Barnsdale? Because you had a scheme. I don't know what it was, nor do I care. But somehow, you were going to stop the flight. You may be a rank amateur, but you had your priorities right. Now, you dare not make a move.'

'I can still get you afterwards, George.'

'Without evidence? Trusted by nobody? And I'm sure you realise there will be a certain reticence in some quarters to rake over the whole sad affair.'

'That,' I said, 'I can imagine.'

'Well, then.' He stirred himself. 'Far be it from me to cause you agonies of conscience in the next few days. Who knows but that you might decide to call my bluff and try stopping the flight?'

'I might, at that.'

'In that case, you underestimate me. You wouldn't want to put either lady at risk, would you? I won't embarrass you by asking which of them you cherish most. Just think of them as a double insurance policy for Uncle George.' He helped himself to a second drink. 'You see,' he went on, 'they are quite safe, but in different places. So sad they can't console one another, but I'm careful by nature. Even if you should free yourself—which I doubt; even if you should by some miracle find the one, you will inevitably lose the other.'

'I'm to be given the opportunity?' More and more, the man talked in riddles. 'Why not shoot me and have done with it?'

'As I said,' George complained, 'you're a rank amateur. You have a crude and unsubtle nature. What would I gain by killing you? Peace of mind for the next vital days, perhaps, but in the long term, nothing. I thought I had made that clear.' I could hardly believe his calmness. 'On the other hand,' he went on, 'what would I lose?'

'What *would* you lose?'

'Suppose you disappeared for no good reason; you, a senior civil servant, a talker to the press. What kind of trouble would that stir up? Apart from all else, your well-connected wife would raise hell.'

'She's going to raise hell anyway. Unless you kill her, too.'

'You go from bad to worse. Dispose of you *both*? People would dig very deep indeed if the pair of you went missing.

As for her reaction to the way things have gone, you do me less than justice. I think she'll be grateful.'

'She's not the grateful type.'

'She will be, when she realises you're debarred henceforth from active service, as it were. She wants that, doesn't she?'

I let that one ride. 'If you can't afford to kill us,' I argued, 'what's to stop me walking out?'

'You have it all back to front again, Goddard.' George sounded almost weary. 'I have nothing to gain as long as you behave, but equally I have nothing to *lose* if you put everything at risk. In that case, I would have to cut my losses, would I not? Think about it, my boy.'

'All right,' I said. 'I'll think about it. What happens now?'

'You stay out of sight, that's all.'

'Where?'

'You'll be safe enough. No communications, reasonable comfort, not long to wait.'

'You think I'm going somewhere nice and quiet with a couple of your thugs?'

'You're in no danger, Goddard, I assure you. In fact I wouldn't trust them anywhere near you.'

I heard one of the thugs shift, somewhere behind me.

We drove for something more than an hour. I was in the back of the van and could see nothing, but it seemed to me that we twisted and turned a great deal. Optimists may think they can keep track of their position without any visual reference; I soon accepted that George and his two companions had achieved their object in making me lose all sense of direction and distance. In the end we drove into some kind of garage or shed, and they led me out with no more than a slender torch beam to guide the way.

They had gone to some trouble—though not much—to make me comfortable. The room was windowless, lit by a single electric bulb, and was equipped with a camp bed, a chair, an electric fire and a supply of iron rations. I complained bitterly about the latter, feeling that I had to make a point of something.

'Don't worry, Goddard,' said George. 'You won't starve.

My friends here will be looking after you; they will pass in a hot meal every now and again.'

'Since you're so well equipped with hostages, I'm surprised you find them necessary.'

'Don't be bitter, Goddard. They have been told to look after you. Ministering to your needs may not be their top priority, but they will do their best. More to the point, they will make sure nobody finds you here. They will also, needless to say, gently discourage you from doing anything silly, like making a break for it.'

'Belt and braces, as it were?'

'Absolutely. Make the most of it, man; a few days and it will all be over. I should spend the time working out what you're going to say afterwards. Remember what I told you; fight it, and you achieve nothing.'

I certainly thought a good deal, though not entirely along the lines George had suggested. He surely didn't expect me to waste time thinking about next week, rather than my present position? It was difficult to tell. He was tightly under control, working up to the climax of his scheme. If I threatened him with failure, I judged he would prove utterly desperate; that his threat to Liz and Jean was real.

With that as a starting point, I was driven to wonder whether I should make any move at all. Why should I try to save Arthur Morland from the results of his own stupidity? Why should I worry about Morland Aircraft, when the firm was clearly past caring about me as anything but a threat to their existence? It would be so easy to take the rest, to return to life afterwards, to learn with surprise that the second President had crashed after all.

It would be easy, except that Morland would have a flight test crew with him. It would be easy, except that I was damned if Simpson—and the people above Simpson—was going to win. It would be easy, except for Jean. I could accept George's point about Liz being grateful if things turned out his way, but Jean would never go along with the idea of burying the whole affair, of accepting that we had been beaten. It mattered a great deal to me what

Jean would think, afterwards. Always assuming there *was* an afterwards.

They did at least provide hot meals at irregular intervals. I found that doubly depressing. The irregularity prevented my forming any definite plan, and the fresh cooking, grim though it was, meant that my guardians were encamped close at hand. There seemed only to be the two of them, but their door-opening technique was well-drilled and foolproof. They stayed far apart, one always covering the other.

I had to concentrate to keep track of time. It may not have been George's intention, though he may have accepted it as a bonus, but the permanent artificial light had the effect of mild brain-washing. The standard counter was to divide the day rigidly into periods of activity and relaxation —to devise a schedule. It was this that led me to inspect the room even more closely than I might otherwise have done.

The place was certainly blessed with either isolation or good soundproofing. No matter how many hearty yells I gave, there was no reaction, not even from the two guardians of the gate. It seemed unlikely that they would have resisted the temptation to tell me I could scream my head off, so I presumed they were out of earshot. That was my first vestige of encouragement.

The door of the room was metal, and very strong. They bolted and locked it each time they left, and I didn't waste all that much time examining its possibilities. They were non-existent. The floor was of solid concrete, with no drainage covers or openings of any description. I might have had more hope for the ceiling, were it not for the lack of anything substantial on which to stand, for it was a good ten feet clear of the floor.

That left the walls, which were uniformly plastered and none too clean. I started off by sounding them, without any rewarding hollowness becoming apparent. After that I unshipped one of the supports from my camp bed and dug away at the plaster to see what was underneath. The wall containing the door, and that opposite the door, turned out to be of concrete as solid as the floor. When I scraped the side walls, however, I was rewarded with a glimmer of hope.

The material I uncovered, low down in the corner where I hoped it would not be noticed, was breeze block—low-density grey stuff, roughly cemented. Now, most people have an exaggerated idea of the strength of ordinary building construction, based partly on ignorance and partly on a sense of respect for property. The fact remains that a determined man of average size and fitness can knock a hole in a single-web brick wall unaided, and I reckoned breeze block should be easier than brick. Besides, I was a good deal bigger than average.

The timing was the difficult thing, but I now knew I could reckon on a lengthy interval between visits. George might have told his two thugs to look after me, but they were in no way inclined to be sociable. I decided to wait half an hour after they had delivered one of their execrable meals, and then start work.

It was as well I didn't start at once, because half an hour later I was honoured with a visit from George. He followed in the larger of the guardians, waited while the man set down the plate, and looked carefully around him. I hoped it was force of habit, and prayed he would fail to notice the places where I had been scraping away the plaster.

'Behaving yourself, I hear?' he said.

'How would they know? I only see them twice a day. Not,' I added hastily, 'that I miss them all that much.'

'I doubt if you'll have to put up with them all that much longer,' said George.

'About set to fly, are they?' It was half past five; unless he had left early, which I doubted, we were pretty close to the factory.

'Soon, soon.' George smiled benevolently.

'Tell me,' I countered, 'how do I know you've really got the two girls?'

'You should have asked before now, Goddard, if you thought I was bluffing. Though the answer would have been the same. If you are leading up to a request to see one or both of them, spare yourself the effort. I'm not going to halve my advantage for no good reason, not even for ten minutes. We could always arrange something ingenious like a tape recording of your wife reciting something at your request, but do you really doubt I have them?'

'Not really,' I admitted. 'I only thought it might be interesting to see how quickly you could have produced one or the other.'

'You have a devious mind, Goddard.'

'Yes, haven't I? I'm still working on the problem of dealing with you.'

'You worry me, Goddard.' George didn't sound very worried. 'What have you got against me? Personally, I mean. I've done everything possible to keep you clear of trouble. Arthur Morland hates you; I respect you. He gave you a hearty thump on the back of the head; I'm trying to keep you from any sort of harm. Think about it.'

'I already have.' I let it out grudgingly. He smiled as though to encourage and nurture the thought, and left it alone with me to take root and flower.

I chose my spot with care. The wall would be weakest in the centre, but I wanted to stay as close as possible to the door. In the end I marked a spot some six feet from the junction with the concrete wall and launched myself. I felt it give even as I bounced clear, and a close inspection revealed cracks in the plaster, following the edges of the looser blocks. A second assault served to emphasise the weak points, and in a very short time I was able to ease out the first block and see what lay beyond. I discovered that I was attacking a cavity wall, with asbestos filling the intervening space. Clearly the place had been built as a fireproof store, which at once explained the lack of windows and the good soundproofing.

By degrees I pulled away the first layer of blocks and extracted the asbestos to give me a clear run at the rest of the wall. Twenty minutes after commencing my attack, I was through into the next room.

It was a big disappointment, though I should have expected something of the sort. Apart from a pile of sacking in one corner, it was a twin of the room I had just left, and its door was equally firmly locked. It crossed my mind that I might somehow out-manoeuvre my two guardians if they paid me a visit and found the hole, but it left too much to chance. There was but one daunting alternative, and that was to carry on as I had started, in the hope that the next room might yield an unlocked door or a window.

My assault on the next wall had the confidence born of experience, but was slowed by the state of my unaided shoulder. The inevitable bruising was beginning to cause me considerable pain, and my head, too, throbbed where Arthur Morland had struck it. Even worse, I was working more or less in the dark, for the room was not equipped with an electric bulb and I couldn't reach the one in my original prison to change it over.

The splinters of asbestos worked their way into my hands as I tore at the packing, and it was perhaps half an hour before I was able to strike at the next layer of wall. When the first block fell away with a clatter, I saw nothing but darkness beyond. The light shining through the hole from my original room had a hard enough job illuminating its next door neighbour, and gave me no help at all as I peered into the stygian gloom of the next chamber. There was nothing for it but to enlarge the hole, clamber through and explore by hand. I was, I reflected bitterly, becoming more and more used to that particular technique.

There was nothing to be gained by waiting, so I pushed out three more blocks and eased my front half into the space beyond, feeling for the floor. It caused a fatal lapse in my concentration, because for a second or two I was more worried about arriving without landing in a heap than in looking or listening for any sign of danger. Then something—a whisper of sound, a blacker-than-black whirl of movement—warned me I was not alone, but too late. The throbbing area at the back of my skull exploded in a flood of pain and I knew no more.

With all the practice I had suffered in the art of waking up painfully, I should have made a better job of it on that occasion. A man has his dignity, but I was more concerned with convincing George that he hadn't lost any.

thing and there was no point in harming the girls.

It reminded me very much of waking up in Lovegrove's cellar; I knew full well that I was awake, yet I could see nothing. My world was one of feeling, centred on a new and splitting headache. In the hope that they had left me alone for the time being, I struggled to sit up and saw light for the first time: a vivid red flash with its origins close to my optic nerve. I was horribly sick, and some insanely rational part of my mind recalled that nausea was a common symptom of concussion.

Another, even more lunatic idea was that someone was holding me, supporting me while I was ill. I tried to work out what was really happening but the feeling stayed with me. It took a long time to accept that someone was there, and even longer to sort out the background noise into recognisable words. After that I suffered a total loss of faith, because what I heard was impossible, despite the urgency of the whispering.

'Neil!' It grew louder and more angry. A hand smartly slapped my face and nearly made me pass out again. I swore vividly, and it helped.

'That's better. Can you understand what I say?' She gripped my shoulders and I felt the strength of the fingers as they dug in. 'Do you know who it is?'

'Jean?' I blinked uncertainly, daring to believe at last. 'It *is* Jean?'

'That's right, love. It's me.'

'Well, leave my bloody head alone. If you touch it again, it'll fall off.'

'I'm sorry, Neil. That was my fault.'

'You and Arthur Morland both. What happened?'

'I knocked you out,' she explained needlessly.

It all began to fall together as my head cleared. 'Is there a light?' I asked.

'There is, but I don't want to switch it on. I don't know how long it will be before they come back.'

'You mean they don't know what's happened?'

'Not yet. I heard you thumping away at the wall, and I didn't understand what was happening. All I knew was that somebody was forcing a way through, and I thought if they could get in, I could get out. So when you poked your head through the hole, I hit you. I didn't realise it was you,' she said lamely.

'And then you found you couldn't get out anyway.'

'That's right. But I covered up the hole in the wall of your room as best I could, by dragging the chair in front of it. If they find you've gone, they'll like as not come charging in here to make sure they've still got me, without checking how you escaped. We have to be ready for them when they come.'

I could see the reason for her urgency. 'What if they come here first?' I thought hard, painful though it was.

For ten minutes we prayed they wouldn't come, while we made ready for them. The first move was to make Jean as ghastly a sight as we could, with the aid of her lipstick; after that we fused the lights by the simple expedient of trapping a coin in the socket and switching on. Jean had to stand on my shoulders to manage it, reminding me painfully of how I had found her.

After that, we had no alternative but to wait, and I knew that would prove the hardest part of all.

'Have you been here all this time?' I should have asked her sooner, and felt guilty for my omission.

'I've sort of lost track,' she apologised. 'They brought Liz in once, to make me write a letter . . .'

'I know.'

'They were waiting for us at the flat, Neil. That was the afternoon you flew the President with Arthur Morland. I'd taken Liz over to Pontefract; it wasn't a good choice, because you came right over the top of us when you took off. I don't know whether she guessed, but she seemed pretty angry to me, though she said nothing. When we went back to the flat they were in the living room . . . Liz almost went mad, but underneath it all she was scared. I'm worried about her, Neil, she's too fragile a person to stand very much of this.'

'What about you? You've been on your own for over a week.'

'I'm all right.' In the darkness, she sounded indignant.

'If I'd been fragile, I'd have broken years ago. My upbringing wasn't as sheltered as hers.'

'When they brought her in, did she say anything? Have you no idea where they're keeping her?'

'They wouldn't let her say anything, Neil. She just sat there, and I knew if I didn't write the letter they'd start twisting her arm until I did. It was horrible, much worse than if they had simply threatened me.'

'Did she look all right?'

'Not really, Neil, she looked as miserable as hell. They wouldn't let us bring anything from the flat, just hustled us out of the flat into separate vans. I doubt if Liz has ever been dirty in her life before now.'

'Have they told you nothing? About why they took you, I mean.'

'Not a thing, though I guessed you'd found enough to scare them. What was it?'

'I landed the President in one piece, that's what scared them. They knew I couldn't have done it without working out the whole plot.' I told her how Arthur Morland had put paid to my hopes of immediate action. 'There it is, Jean,' I concluded lamely. 'I know the whole story, and it will do no good at all unless we can get out of here.'

'But what did they do to the President, Neil? It must have been very clever, if it took you all that time to find out.'

'On the contrary, it was childishly simple. Things only seemed complicated because somebody obligingly trailed a red herring for them.'

'Those were the people who put you in the cellar, when I found you?' Jean fished instinctively for the story. 'The people you made the deal with, who gave you back the crash recorders? Who *was* behind that, anyway?'

'A deal's a deal, Jean. I might tell you, one day. But you know who's behind the real thing.'

'No, I don't.'

'You mean George Simpson hasn't been to gloat over you?'

'Of course he has!' Jean sniffed. 'But why would he organise anything like that? He was ideally placed to carry it out, I can see that, but who put him up to it? He could have had no personal motive.'

It was clear that Jean had been doing plenty of thinking on her own account. 'Let's leave it at this,' I said. 'Morlands have annoyed a lot of people in Whitehall. They wouldn't indulge in sabotage, oh no, but they'd be mightily glad if somebody did. And some of their keener subordinates have a strange sense of duty.'

'I don't believe it,' she said, fishing for the rest of the story.

'Remember Thomas à Becket? Who will rid me of this turbulent aircraft manufacturer? Or something like that.'

'But if that was all they wanted, why couldn't they have left the original scheme to go ahead?'

'Because theirs was better. The first scheme depended on a bomb cutting the elevator control circuit. Now, if you blow something up, a careful chemical analysis will always give it away. Of course, it was quite a cunning scheme; they linked the detonator circuit through the flap blowing switch...'

'What's flap blowing?' interrupted Jean.

'Heavens, woman, what would your father say? You take air from the engine compressors and squirt it over the wing flaps, then you can fly slower without falling out of the sky.'

'I see,' she encouraged meekly.

'Good. Wiring up the bomb like that meant it would only go off when the President was flying its final approach, you see? And that in turn meant it would almost certainly crash nose-first...'

'Why?' said Jean, but I ignored her.

'...and if it did, the elevator circuit would be totally mangled; or so they hoped. Equally important, they had a good idea where it would crash, enabling them to station people ready to pick up the crash recorders in case they gave anything away.'

'But that was bad thinking, wasn't it? Because by taking the recorders they made it obvious that something was wrong.'

'Not obvious, no. People shy away from sabotage as an explanation for any crash. On balance they were right, because if their scheme *had* worked, the recorders probably would have given it away.'

'And as it was, the recorders didn't help, because there was no bomb. Is that what you're saying?'

'Absolutely. Simpson's people took out the bomb. Their scheme was much better, virtually undetectable. That was essential, because their aim was to finish Morlands as aircraft builders. The first lot only wanted Morlands' shares to dip for a week or two.'

'How did Simpson find out about the bomb plot?'

'You said it yourself, Jean. George Simpson was ideally placed. He's a bloody good security man. He must have known about the bomb for some time, and let it ride in case their guilty consciences should prove useful. They very nearly did.'

'How was that, then?' She was entirely serious now.

'Well, George—I assume it was George—fed me a clue about the bomb plot, and I followed it up. It all hung together, so I set up an elaborate scheme to try and stampede them, by making it look as though we'd found something in the remains of the elevator circuit. George was out-thinking me all along the line at that point. The bomb plotters panicked and grabbed me, and somehow George fed them the line that Morlands *still* weren't sure what had happened.'

'I don't follow.'

'Neither did they, luckily. George's idea was that they should get rid of the evidence...'

'You mean, get rid of you?'

'Exactly. Instead, their man tried to find out who I'd told and what the evidence consisted of. I told him the truth; he took a while to swallow it, but soon enough realised what a wonderful double-cross somebody had pulled. So they did their deal with me and faded quietly from the scene.'

'But what *was* the scheme, Neil? Simpson's one, I mean.'

'It all hinged on one good idea, and the system Morlands —or anyone else—uses to design and build an aeroplane. If you look at the President's electrical system, what have you got?'

'Miles and miles of wire, I expect.'

'That's right. All running between switches and motors and instruments and goodness knows what else. Anyway, Simpson found somebody to work out a way of switching the wires to obtain the desired effect. It was supremely clever because it used all existing wiring, nothing had to be added; but the result of simply switching terminals was catastrophic.'

'Go on.' Jean sounded absorbed, and I knew it was all being filed away in her memory. There was no reason why not.

'In a nutshell, they arranged it so that when the wheels were down and the flap blowing was on, the elevator gearing was reduced and the trim sense reversed.'

'I'm sorry,' she said. 'That's just gibberish.'

'You should have listened a bit harder to MacPherson,' I said, and a fist came out of the darkness and thumped me, hard.

'It's like this,' I explained carefully. 'The elevator needs to be geared so that you end up with very small movements at high speed, to stop the aircraft being torn apart, and much larger movements at low speed so that the pilot has a good margin of control on the approach. Is that clear?'

'So far, yes.'

'Right, then. The *trim* is the system the pilot uses for balancing out the load on his control column. In some aircraft it just changes the spring loading in the control circuit, but in the President there is a motor which moves the whole tailplane.'

'Is that important?'

'Vital. Imagine you're flying the President. You turn finals, and lower full flap, at which point the flap blowing comes on automatically. Because of the wiring change, the elevator gearing unit starts to gear down. You don't notice at first, because you're concentrating very hard on the runway and anyway the thing doesn't happen at once, it motors over quite slowly, nibbling away at your margin of con-

trol. Then you realise you haven't much forward stick movement in hand.'

'So you go round and try again?'

'Unfortunately, no. You trim forward, trying to take the
load off the column and give yourself some more forward
movement to play with.'

'But they had reversed the trim!'

'That's right. Instead of what you expect, the nose carries
on rising and there's nothing you can do about it, because
you already have the wheel jammed fully forward. So you
pile on the power to see if that makes any difference, and
for John Rose that only made things worse. By then, you
see, the nose was so high that the President was pushed into
a low-speed loop.'

'But you got away with it, Neil.'

'Only just. I was *expecting* something to happen. Even so,
I might not have spotted it had not Arthur Morland been
in such a flat panic that I looked across to see what he was
up to. It was a closer run thing than I ever want to live
through again, and not helped by having to fight off Arthur
at the same time.'

'So then you knew what they had done?' Jean was very
good at prodding along a narrative at a steady pace.

'Well, it all started to piece together. The penny really
dropped when I hoisted the flaps and the stick motored
smartly back to clout me in the crutch. With the flaps up,
you see, the trim went back to normal, and the sudden re-
versal almost crashed us even as I worked it out.'

'That doesn't explain it all, does it?'

'Why not?' More than anything, I put it that way to see
if her clear mind could pinpoint anything I'd forgotten.

'Why wasn't it found during the ground tests?' she asked.
'And why didn't you spot it when you flew the flight test
programme? Surely you tried landing on a cloud or something, isn't that what you're supposed to do? And apart
from that, how did they change the terminals without being noticed by anyone in the hangar?' I was reminded
how much that would matter to Jean, since her father was
ultimately responsible.

'You have it back to front, girl. The way they organised

it was to prepare a different drawing for issue to the hangars. It had the same number, it was drawn—I think—by the same man; they even amended it each time it was re-issued with changes. The drawing in the hangar was never the same as the one in the drawing office, but the system was supposed to be foolproof, so nobody ever checked.'

'Then the people in the hangar ...' she faltered.

'... worked to the drawing in all good faith, and set the whole thing up for them. Now, for those other points. Getting through the ground checks undetected depended on two things. One was the cleverness of the wiring changes; the other was the influence the people concerned had on the ground test schedule. Remember that their scheme only worked in one particular set of circumstances. They had arranged things well enough, for instance, for everything to work normally when the President was standing on the ground. Some checks are naturally run with the aircraft on jacks, but they were able to avoid a situation where the wheels were raised, then lowered again, before the flap blowing switch was tried.'

'They could do all that?'

'In the President, yes. Raising the undercarriage resets two switches, both of which have spare terminals.'

'So they went undetected during the ground checks. What about the flight? The undercarriage would have been up and down by then.'

'That was easy. The flight test programme called for a check of approach characteristics at ten thousand feet. They simply wired through one of the five-thousand-foot switches in the pressurisation circuit.'

'And you spotted none of the changes in the wreckage?'

'How could we, Jean? We were checking the whole thing by drawings from the hangar store, weren't we? The very drawings that had been used to build in the changes to begin with. There was only one point at which the whole thing nearly fell apart.'

'When was that?'

'When the bomb plotters broke into the hangar to try and make sure there was no evidence against them. Remember *they* had worked from the flap blowing microswitch, so they replaced the one that was in the wreckage with one that was wired up as it should have been.'

'You mean, as it should have been according to the drawing office?'

'Exactly. That meant it was *wrong* according to the hangar drawing, which was why George—or one of his minions—had to go in the following night and replace it in turn with one wired up to the hangar drawing. That was a close shave, because if anyone had really checked the switch that day, rather than simply making sure it was still there, it would have blown the whole scheme wide apart.'

Jean moved against me. 'It's incredible,' she said. 'Four people dead—six, nearly—and all for what?'

'I'd rather leave you to work that one out. Somewhere, some day, you'll maybe meet a man who says look, Morlands were selling military aircraft to the wrong people, they had to be stopped and they had exhausted the legal possibilities of doing so. What will you say to him?'

'I don't know.' She leaned her head on my shoulder. 'What would you say?'

'I'm just hoping I never meet him. Do you think these blasted people are going to make another appearance?'

'I wish you hadn't done that,' she said gently.

'Done what?'

'Dragged me back to the present. I don't think they will come, not now. Not until morning.'

'Oh dear. Shall I retire gracefully until then?'

'You dare,' said Jean.

# ◢17◣

By the time they came, we were ready for them. Indeed, we had been ready for two hours, Jean sprawled on the bed and me behind the door. I had no definite plan of campaign, not knowing what they would do or even which room they would visit first. At least, I thought, I would have the advantage of eyes attuned to darkness by twelve hours without light.

They came for Jean first. There was a rattle at the door as the bolts were withdrawn and the key turned in the lock, and I could feel my heartbeat and blood pressure going up. Then the door swung open, admitting a dim shaft of light from the corridor beyond, and the wavering beam of a torch. As I had hoped, we had fused the electrical system of the whole building.

The man behind the torch tried the light switch inside the door—a natural but useless gesture—and then searched for Jean with his torch. His muttered oath as it found her came sharply through the stillness. She was an unnerving sight, lying on her back with her head and one arm over the edge. A bright red stain ran from one corner of her open mouth and round her throat. The torch beam was too narrow to pick it all up at once, but it had the desired effect. The man rushed forward, calling to his companion who, as on all previous occasions, had hovered outside the door.

The second man almost spoiled it, for he moved inside but not across to Jean. I wanted the two of them close together, but it was now plain that simultaneous disposal was out of the question. Lacking any suitable weapon, the only thing I could do was step behind the man at the door and put my full weight behind a punch at his kidneys. It was a partial success in that it stopped him dead, but he took a long time dropping and I stumbled over him as I made for the bed. The torch flashed round and caught me square in the eyes, and the shock of so much concentrated light caused me real physical pain. There was a scuffling noise and a grunt of surprise, and suddenly I felt his hands scrabbling for my ankles. It was a natural reaction to kick out, and I made sickening contact with the toe of my right shoe.

He made no sound, and I thought for a moment that it was all over, until he managed to grab my ankle anyway and bring me down. I fell on my bruised shoulder, doing nothing for my presence of mind, and somehow he got on top of me. His hands reached for my neck, and I was certain he had forgotten any stricture from George about keeping me in reasonable condition. Despite the absence of light I began to see flashes of colour, and the conviction came that it was a bad fight to be losing. Then the hands jerked and loosened for no apparent reason. As my senses pulled themselves together there came a nasty crunch, and this time my assailant toppled sideways and lay still.

The torch flashed on, lighting his head. It was a mess, not only facially where I had kicked him, but at the back of his skull. I sat up gingerly, making sure he was out cold.

'What the hell did you hit him with?' I asked unsteadily.

'The torch. It was all there was.' Jean sounded very matter-of-fact about it all. I reached out and took the torch. It was a fine strong one, and weighed a good couple of pounds. She was lucky not to have killed him. As it was, his breathing was far from good, but I hoped he would survive. The other man was awake, but locked in a spasm of agony. A search revealed the gun he had waved at me from outside the door when his companion was bringing my meals.

Jean was still kneeling by the side of the first man. I moved across and dragged her to her feet. 'No time for that,' I complained. 'For a starter, let's find out where we are.'

'What are you going to do, Neil?' She was back to being practical.

I looked at my watch. 'It's not yet eight o'clock. What time does your father go to work?'

'He'll be on his way by now, Neil. I could try getting in touch with him at the factory. Is that what's worrying you? That nobody there will listen to you?'

'They won't even give me the chance to speak, you know that. My idea was to persuade your father to re-wire the aircraft correctly, but I guess it's too late for that now.' I locked the door and put the key in my pocket. Jean flashed the torch along the corridor. It stretched both ways into the gloom. 'At least,' I said, 'we'll have time to think of something. They won't fly the aircraft until much later in the day, even assuming George was right about the flight being today.' The floor of the corridor was covered in a strange mixture of concrete and coal dust, crunching under our feet. The beam of the torch revealed the filth of the walls.

We turned a corner, and saw daylight for the first time, creeping under the doors of the garage or loading bay in which we found ourselves. The place was empty; our two friends either had a hideout close at hand, or they were delivered by something which dumped them and drove off. I found the catch on the massive doors and swung them open.

For me, the sight was a strange one. The overwhelming impression was one of dirt and decay. A concreted yard stretched away in front of us, broken here and there by rusty railway lines.. It ended up at the foot of a massive grey hill of weather-worn slag. As I turned, it seemed that the spoil heaps rose all round us, cutting off the view in every direction. What a place, I thought, for George to have secreted us. No wonder he had seemed so unconcerned about the chances of our being found.

Unfortunately, our surroundings gave no clue as to where we were. Coal mines, active or abandoned, covered so much of the area around Barnsdale that we could have been anywhere within a hundred square miles.

'Neil!' exclaimed Jean from beside me, 'the tower.' She pointed to a massive structure which had clearly been used for loading coal into railway wagons, a mess of conveyors and hoppers and girders, rising from amongst the slag like a skeletal skyscraper. It must have been a good hundred feet high, and a series of ladders ran to its topmost levels.

I was not in my best climbing form that morning, my shoulder was far from recovered from its use as a battering ram, and I made slow progress up the first five landings. The slag heaps had an infuriating trick of seeming just as high however fast one climbed, and it was not until we were a good sixty feet up—Jean, I saw with alarm, kept up with no trouble—that I felt the spur to rush the rest of the way.

Our surroundings must have blocked sound as well as sight, because the roar came to me by degrees. As I realised its import I forgot about the pain in my legs and the struggling of my lungs. The next four landings passed almost unnoticed, and the fifth one totally so, because suddenly we were presented with a panoramic view over the grey slag tops with their dark inset mirrors of old slurry beds. Everything fell into place. The airfield lay on both sides of us. The long runway of North Field gleamed as I squinted into the low sun of the winter morning; the jumble of massive buildings around South Field reflected back at me where the light caught the frost on their walls.

It was a magnificent morning, almost a freak by Barnsdale standards. The clear blue stretched from horizon to horizon in one unbroken arc, and the visibility was unlimited. It was the sort of morning when one aches to go flying, and with that thought came the awful realisation. The noise which had brought me scrambling up was thrown once more into focus. I was barely conscious of Jean beside me, clutching my arm.

A cloud of smoke rose, away at the eastern end of the North Field runway. A few seconds later came the thunder, and then the slender white shape launched itself out of the sun. The nose lifted as it came abreast of us, and it eased smoothly off the ground.

'Oh, Neil,' breathed Jean. 'It's the President, isn't it?'

We half galloped, half slid down the flights of stairs, only to stand indecisively when we reached the ground.

'So much for boxing clever,' I said. 'Assuming he's flying

the same schedule, we've got an hour to stop him crashing the thing.'

'Are you sure it's Arthur Morland flying it?'

'Would it make any difference if it wasn't? He's flying it all right. That turn after lift-off was too flamboyant for it to be anyone else.'

'Can you convince them at the main gate? Will they let you in?'

'They'll just have to, Jean.' My mind was turning over at high speed, but thinking far from clearly. I took her by the hand and we ran in the direction of Morlands' main gate, hard by the colliery entrance. I remembered Jack Old telling me that the mine had been closed after causing too many subsidences in the runways.

Fortunately, the man wasn't expecting us, otherwise the whole thing might have come to an end at that point. His job was to keep people out rather than us in; he came wandering out at the sound of running footsteps and stood wondering just long enough for me to work it out and dive off the main track into the piles of slag. There was a shout, and he came running in his turn. That suited me fine. Unless he was very bright, we would soon outflank him and make it out of the gate.

In some ways, it was not my morning. He was bright enough to realise that his primary task was to guard the gate. Not only that, he was armed and apparently prepared to shoot. My first warning of this came when I looked round the corner of a decrepit hut near the gate and was rewarded with a bullet much too close for comfort.

'That settles it,' I whispered to Jean, who was crouched behind me. 'We'll have to find another way out.'

'I don't think it'll do any good,' she said. 'These places are properly fenced in. Apart from the danger of somebody falling down a shaft, it's a perfect place for overlooking Morlands. The wire will keep us in just as surely as it keeps most people out.'

'Either we do that, or we find a way past him,' I pointed out. 'Arthur's had ten minutes already.'

'What about that gun?' said Jean.

I looked at the weapon I was holding. 'A shooting match?

It's no better than an even chance. I'd waste time trying to manoeuvre into a good position, and if he has a spare magazine I could end up in big trouble. Over the fence is better, if it's at all possible.' I peered carefully round the corner and found my new opponent making his way towards us. There was no point in letting him get too close, so I slipped the safety catch off my gun and fired one round in his general direction. He went to ground in a way which showed great faith in my ill intentions, and I saw him working his way back out of effective pistol range. His object was still clearly to guard the gate and stop us getting out at all costs. I wondered if he had a telephone with which to get in touch with George, and was encouraged to think that George was probably now in the control tower and poorly placed to receive warnings. Another three minutes had ticked by.

Jean eased her position and yelped with alarm as the door of the hut gave behind her. I cursed her for making a noise and giving me a shock, but she only glared back. It was difficult to tell how much cover there was between me and the gate. If we retreated to look at the fence, would he come after us? In his position, I thought, I would follow the policy of least risk and stay where I was, having chosen a safe hiding place with clear approaches. But would we simply waste time trying to find another way out, as Jean seemed to think?

'Neil!' She shook my bad shoulder, and I cursed again. The pressure of evaporating time was playing hell with my nerves. 'What about these?' she said urgently, and I glanced back to see her waving a large and rusty pair of wire cutters, of the massive two-handed kind.

'Where did those come from?' I asked incredulously.

'Inside the hut. The door opened when I stumbled against it, and there they were.'

'What price your fence now?'

'I don't know.' She viewed the cutters critically. 'They haven't been used for ages, and they don't look very sharp.'

'They're still our best chance.' A quick time check showed that twenty minutes had gone already. Arthur Morland would be over the North Sea, up at about twenty thousand feet, able to see most of the way from Hull to Newcastle on such a morning as this. Meanwhile, I thought it well to discourage the man at the gate, in case he decided to come and investigate. I told Jean to stay put, and ran from cover to cover towards him. It was impossible to approach very close without being seen, and he was a cool enough customer, though not actually keen on seeing the whites of my eyes. At fifty yards' range he pinned me down with three spaced shots, and I ventured two in return. Fifty yards is a hopeless distance for short-barrelled pistols, but I did the best I could. He would sit tight for a bit.

The mine area was a bigger place than I had realised. We threaded our way through the slag for a fair distance and twice found ourselves in dead-ends, short of climbing the steep-sided heaps. Eventually we emerged in another open yard, crossed a railway track and reached the fence at last. There was nothing beyond except some rough grass, dipping into a cutting which I knew contained the mineral railway serving to divide North and South Fields. On the far side of the cutting, a second fence betrayed the airfield boundary. There was no road, not even a path outside the fence, but at least that meant we would be spared interference while we cut our way out. Nearly half an hour had gone. Arthur would be checking his fuel, and running some more checks on the approach characteristics—at ten thousand feet. Even so, I was sure he would be checking with considerable care.

The cutters were almost disastrously blunt. I could imagine some maintenance engineer throwing them down in disgust in the last days before the mine closed, to rust away in the hut. But they cut the wire, strand by strand, opening a two-foot hole for us to crawl through. The wire was tough, plastic-coated steel, and the jaws of the cutter slipped when I applied pressure. It was almost a case of having to saw through each time. Eventually I was able to fold back a flap of wire and wriggle through, dragging Jean behind me. My watch said the President had been airborne nearly forty minutes. That meant it would be turning for home. I set off at a run, back towards the main gate.

'Neil!' Jean practically shrieked. I turned; she hadn't even started to run after me. 'Stop!' she cried. 'Have you no sense at all?'

Her anger pulled me up with a start. 'What else can we do?' I demanded. 'Sit here for a grandstand view of the crash?'

'You bloody fool.' There was more than a hint of exasperation in her voice. She looked even taller than usual, and the first hint of a wind came from the west and fluttered her skirt as she stood there. Her dignity transcended the awful state of her face, from which she had managed to remove only the worst of the lipstick stain.

'What are you going to do?' she asked scornfully. 'Run for the main gate. But the factory main gate is next to the mine entrance, isn't it? Right beside your friend with the gun. How do you rate your chances of getting through in one piece?'

'So you're thinking quicker than me.' Jean and I were getting to the stage where there was no need to spell everything out. 'Stop trying to prove how much brighter you are,' I said, 'and tell me what *you* think we should do.' Even as we argued, the seconds were ticking away for Arthur Morland.

'If the main gate let you in, where would you go?'

'The control tower, of course.'

'And what's that?' She pointed dramatically, unable to resist the build-up even in such an emergency.

Four hundred yards away, as if in answer to a signal, the sun caught one of the slanting glass panels of the Morland control tower, squatting on the grass beside the main runway.

'Another thing,' panted Jean as she wriggled through our second hard-won hole, 'where do you think George will be?'

'In the tower,' I said foolishly, and saw what she meant. Had we tried the main gate, they would have alerted George. Our direct attack stood a good chance of taking him unawares—unless one of his perimeter security teams spotted us. Come what may, we were through. I was about to look once more at my watch when I realised something else was setting our schedule. A gleaming speck in the sky, the President drifted in from the east, still quite high but pulling round to rejoin the circuit. From now on, every minute counted.

The best people run the quarter-mile in well under a minute, but it took us nearer two before we reached the tower. The dew was still heavy and the grass long, slowing us down a good deal. Jean stumbled twice, the second time leaving her shoes behind. There was no cover, we simply risked all in a straight-line dash. We nearly made it.

My hope was that everyone on the airfield would be looking at the returning President, but George had trained his men better than that. Two of them came bouncing across the tussocky grass in a Land Rover, moving to cut off our line of advance. We were no more than fifty yards short of our objective. I looked up, and saw the aircraft describing a white arc across the line of the runway, still losing height. My mind raced ahead. Downwind in one minute; turn base leg at two minutes and a bit; finals in less than four minutes, crash in six. Unless we could do something. There was surely no time to explain to the security boys, so I didn't try.

In response to my panted advice, Jean broke away, taking a line to bring her round the back of the Land Rover. I kept on going, hoping to persuade them to split forces, and I was successful. One of them jumped out as the vehicle slowed, and ran after Jean; the driver spun his steering wheel and moved to cut me off. I dodged him a couple of times, as one can so easily do when a tightly-turning vehicle is doing the chasing, but my real aim was to infuriate the driver sufficiently to tempt him to jump out without looking too hard.

The third time round, he did exactly as I wanted. I stopped dead just aft of his cab, and he swung out of the door and straight into the muzzle of the gun. It wasn't a nice thing to do, but with five minutes to go I had no real alternative. He pulled up short with one foot still on the door sill, and I knew he would reach for the radio if he was given the chance. I wondered if he even recognised me.

My single shot killed several birds at once. It smashed the radio, convinced my man I meant business, and prompted his companion to let go of Jean. She came and stood dutifully behind me, well out of the way while I sized them up.

'No good,' I said sadly. 'They'll have to come with us.'

'Where are you going?' asked the Land Rover driver.

'Control tower. On the double, unless you want to see a nasty accident.'

They were not to be blamed for placing the wrong interpretation on my threat, but they took me at my word. We ran, all four of us, across to the control tower door. A last glance showed the President fearfully far downwind, practically turning base leg. The wheels were down.

There was no point in trusting the security men on the stairs. It takes more skill than I have to pilot two determined prisoners from one floor to the next, and I had no intention of getting kicked down a couple of flights and losing the whole game at this stage. Jean obediently searched for a room with a key in the lock while I stood guard. It took her another precious half-minute, but she came up with a windowless storage closet; the door wasn't very strong, but the place made up for it by being so small as to leave no room for a charge.

'I'm not going in there,' said the driver from the Land Rover, casting a sideways glance through the door. I cursed inwardly; he was picking an awkward time to be brave and decide I was unwilling to fire.

'If he won't get in,' came a clear voice from beside me, 'shoot him. You've no other choice now, have you?' The man stared at Jean and believed her. He backed inside, and the other followed. Without her, I was painfully aware, I would never have made it. She turned the key in the lock, and we made for the stairs. Our footsteps echoed through the building as we climbed, but there was nobody to hear. All the staff were in the topmost glasshouse, watching the President on its final approach.

My first object on entering the upper level was to establish my position before anyone could react. It was easy enough;

Arthur Morland was contributing to his own salvation by holding their attention riveted as he straightened out on the final approach. There was an air of tension, of expectancy among those present, and several seconds passed before they realised exactly what had happened. By that time, Jean had locked the door and was standing against it.

We were not a pretty sight, but that was probably to our advantage. There were some twenty people in the glass-walled room, and as many more on the balcony outside, but I was only interested in two of them. George Simpson was the first to wake up and move, perhaps inevitably, and he forced my hand by making for Jean. With her as a shield, he might just have managed something. I had an infinite respect for the speed and originality of his thinking, so I shot him as he moved clear of the other spectators.

It is not easy to shoot anyone in cold blood. Even though it was George, and even though I was aiming for his legs, I had to force myself to pull the trigger. But it worked; the bullet took him in the left thigh, and from the way he collapsed it must have broken the bone. The shot froze the quiver of movement among the others, as I had hoped.

'No more heroes,' I warned. 'I don't care who's next,' I added untruthfully. 'Sir William; tell Arthur to take it round before he kills himself.'

Sir William Morland towered incoherently. I could imagine all manner of thoughts chasing themselves around his mind, and he could do no better than stutter, 'Before he *what*?'

'Arthur is about to have a nose-up elevator runaway. Tell him to go round before you lose him.' I squinted out of the window; the President loomed larger. 'It's happening *now*,' I insisted. 'He already has full flap on.'

Sir William stood there stunned, like everyone else. 'Christ,' I burst out, 'can none of you take it in? Give me a microphone, quick.' One of the controllers made a move.

'Give him nothing.' Morland's voice had recovered itself and turned to a deadly growl. 'I'll see you in hell before you talk Arthur into the ground. I'll get you, and your boss, and your bloody Minister, if it comes to that. You're a wrecker, you want to see us finished, and now you've proved you'll stop at nothing to do it. Wasn't it enough to knock my boy senseless so that you could try to damage the aircraft beyond repair?' He turned to watch the President. 'You'll have to shoot me down to reach the console,' he declared, and I knew he meant it. 'Watch this, Goddard,' he said. 'Watch this aeroplane make its first perfect landing. I'll accord you that pleasure before I tear you to pieces.'

I looked desperately around the little group. Most of the faces were ones I knew. Bates, Old; they were pale and shocked. A stream of muttered curses came from George Simpson. The shock and pain had unhinged him as he lay there, and he was bleeding heavily.

'Three miles finals.' It crackled out of the loudspeaker, cutting across the electric atmosphere. When would Arthur realise he was running out of control, and what would he do? Would some miracle remind him what had happened in that last hectic flight?

'You bloody-minded old bastard,' I stormed, full of anger at his supreme folly. 'Your firm can go to hell for all I care.' I tossed him the gun, and he caught it clumsily. As a studied gesture, it might have been managed better; I might have slipped on the safety catch, for instance. Mercifully, it didn't go off. 'I needed that,' I went on, 'to make sure I got a hearing. Now, I don't care whether you listen or not. In about half a minute young Arthur will be at the bottom of a hole in the ground, and you'll have only yourself to blame for the rest of your life. Yourself,' I added bitterly, 'and George Simpson, who set it all up.'

'You've a fine line in talk, Goddard.' The old bastard was digging his heels in, but he was shaken at finding himself holding the gun.

'So have you. God, how easy do you think it *is* to write off an aircraft without writing off yourself as well? Did it never occur to you to question Arthur's story of the second flight? To ask whether there wasn't another explanation to fit the facts?'

'Alfa One,' said the loudspeaker, 'two miles finals.'

'Any minute now,' I warned.

'Say nowt!' snapped Morland as the controller made to

speak. 'Give it another half minute,' he growled. 'Let's see how this thing turns out.'

My blood suddenly ran cold. The old boy was going to let Arthur in really deep. To see if I was right? I had a vision of him telling me it was make or break for Arthur. Was he setting up the rack on which to break him, and did he fully realise the risk?

'He panicked last time,' I warned. 'If you let things go too far, he'll panic again.'

'Let him. That's his look out.'

'It's your thirty million quid,' I protested. 'And your company.' The President was already slightly higher than it should have been for a good approach.

'Very well.' The steel-blue eyes fixed me. 'You say when it's gone far enough.'

'It already has.' Not only was the aircraft above the glidepath, the nose was visibly rising.

'Tell him to take it round.' Morland nodded at the controller.

'Alfa One, this is Morland Tower.' There was a tightness in the man's voice which matched his frown. 'Suggest you go round again, you are a little high.'

The seconds ticked by and the nose went up, but the loudspeaker remained obstinately silent except for the hiss of background noise.

'Alfa One, round again!' This time, an order.

'I can't *hold* it!' At last, the cry of agony.

'Tell him to trim back,' I said. 'Otherwise he'll do the same as John Rose.'

'Trim back, Alfa One.' The controller was fully convinced that I knew what I was talking about.

'*Help* me ...' The words were wrung out of the loudspeaker.

The huge figure dashed forward and grabbed the microphone from the controller's hand. 'Arthur!' rapped Sir William. 'You snivelling little wretch; trim back, back, back!'

The psychology of it was right. The only thing which could now pull Arthur back from the abyss of panic was the long-respected voice of ultimate authority. The rest of us just watched the big white aircraft as it climbed as though aiming to cross the runway threshold at a thousand feet. It was still losing speed.

'I'll not tell you twice, Arthur.' The old man was calm, alone among us. He might have been threatening to thrash Arthur for not being in bed by nine. 'Trim back, open the throttles and overshoot.' He glanced across at me. 'Should he raise the flaps?'

'Not now,' I said, grateful for the recognition. 'He'll stall straight in if he does.'

The President was getting on for forty degrees nose-up before we realised she had stabilised. The smoke trails from the engines grew thicker. Still the aircraft seemed to hover, but at least it didn't fall out of the sky.

'Who's with him up there?' It seemed absurd not to have thought of it before.

'He's solo.' Jack Old pulled himself together and spoke up for the first time.

'You're joking.'

'He didn't want anybody else. And nobody was very keen to go with him, come to that.'

'You all want your brains testing!' I could appreciate the strain they had been under, but it had been manifestly absurd to send Arthur off on his own on this bright winter morning. 'Now we've got to get him down, and it isn't going to be easy.' The President had climbed high enough to vanish from view. We could tell from the craned necks on the balcony outside that it was still gaining height as it crossed the airfield.

'Tell him what to do, Goddard.' Morland thrust the microphone at me. I took it unwillingly.

'Alfa One,' I called, 'this is Zulu One.'

'Goddard!' Arthur was not so far gone as to forget that callsign. 'You can't reach me now,' he said. 'It's all mine now.'

'Arthur, will you do as I say?' Sweet reason seemed the most hopeful approach.

'Go away. It's mine, I tell you.' Morland started forward but I waved him away.

'All right, Arthur. Fly it your own way. Do you fancy

166

another approach like the last? Sort yourself out, I'm through trying to help you.' There was a long silence, unbroken either in the tower or on the radio. Away to the west, towards the Pennines, I could see the President still climbing flat out. 'Christ,' I said. 'He'll be carving his way through the airways in a minute. Better warn Preston; if he collides with a BEA flagship we're sunk.' That was one worry; the other was Arthur's fuel state.

'Arthur,' I tried again, 'where are you going now?'

'Round again.' The answer sounded almost confident.

'Fine. Check your speed and altitude, clean up and start your joining checks.' There was another long silence. Only the smoke trails now betrayed the President's position.

'Zulu One,' came the call, 'Zulu One; what shall I do?'

The sigh of relief went all round the tower, though I thought it premature. 'Speed, Alfa One?' I called.

'Two-ten.'

'Fine. Bring in the flaps.' If he didn't, he would pretty soon have them off. 'Watch out for a hefty trim change,' I warned him hastily. The smoke trail wriggled, far to the west. 'Now throttle back,' I said, 'turn left on to one-zero-zero and check your fuel state.'

'I have three thousand pounds only, Zulu One...'

'Don't worry.' I was doing enough worrying for both of us. 'Stay throttled back, you have plenty of height for a nice long descent.'

'Roger, Zulu One. Can you see me?'

'Yes, Alfa One, we have you in sight.' Just about, that was. But he had turned towards us as requested.

'Neil,' said a half-heard voice, 'what about Liz?' What about her, indeed? We had Simpson, but would he have left instructions for dealing with Liz if anything went wrong?

'See to George. He'll have to tell us where she is. If he won't, kick his leg.' It was one massive problem too many. 'Let those two out from downstairs before they suffocate,' I ordered, 'and let me get on with this, for goodness' sake!'

'Goddard.'

Would they never leave me alone to talk down Arthur? This time it was Sir William. 'Who's *she*?' he said, indicating Jean.

'I'm sorry. Miss Partington, of the *Barnsdale Echo*.' I only said it to scare him, but he nearly blew his top.

'I don't understand you, Goddard,' he complained as he simmered down. 'You drag us out of trouble, and kick us straight back in by turning up with a journalist in tow. What's the idea?'

'The idea is that she, like me, knows it all. Don't worry; her father is your Superintendent in Number Five.'

'Your father works here?' Sir William fixed Jean with his gaze as she knelt beside George. She had found a first aid box somewhere.

'Yes,' she said calmly, out-staring him. I knew he would have to give in, whatever his first instincts. Sir William had more sense than to bribe or threaten.

'You never said,' he grumbled. 'She knows it all, you say; does she know what's at stake here?'

'Indeed she does, just as well as I do.' Thanks to the splendid visibility, we could see the descending President coming in from the west. Half of me flew with Arthur, and struggled with the half which had to explain to Sir William. 'George Simpson set it all up,' I insisted. 'He had my wife and Miss Partington as hostages, and when things warmed up he grabbed me as well.'

'But why'd he do it? And what happens now?' Morland, back on balance, wasted no time in asking the basic questions.

'He did it because he was put up to it; I'm still not sure how. As for what happens, the police—the authorities in general—know nothing. It's largely up to you whether we can keep it that way, you're the man with the connections. Right now, there are only two loose ends.'

'Which are?'

'Finding my wife, and getting Arthur down in one piece. George will help us with the first, and I'd appreciate it if you'd let me get on with the second.'

'Very well.' Morland looked round the glass-walled room. 'You all heard that,' he declared. 'I'd much rather you hadn't, but there was no help for it. We'll try and sort this thing out without screaming blue murder; every one of you can best help by forgetting you saw anything this morning bar a perfect flight. You,' he said to the controller, 'call the doctor across from the sick bay. We have to patch up this ... this...' Words failed Morland as he stared down at George. 'By heck, Goddard,' he said, 'he'll tell us where your wife is if I have to twist his bad leg myself.'

'Thanks for the kind thought, but I don't think you'll have to. George knows he's lost.' I glanced at George, who had pulled himself together sufficiently to be aware what was going on. 'On the basis that Morlands won't make a fuss, the worst that can happen to George is a patching-up in a nursing home and a one-way ticket to obscurity. He stands to lose nothing by taking us to Liz.'

'You're right, of course.' Morland sounded unwilling to accept the logic of it. 'What of his masters?'

'We'll take care of them when the time comes. Acting through the appropriate channels, of course.'

'Of course.' Already he was composing their indictment.

'Alfa One,' I said hastily into the microphone, 'level off now.' Arthur had brought the President down to five thousand feet or so, and I suspected that without prompting he would carry on down until the ground stopped him. 'Alfa One,' I went on, 'you must land with half flap and no blowing, do you understand?'

'Roger, Zulu One.' He sounded slightly recovered.

'Alfa One, repeat my instruction.'

'Half flap, no blowing.'

'Alfa One, make your approach speed one-eighty knots, and aim for touchdown at one-sixty. Start your downwind checks now, and take a nice wide sweep round the base leg.'

'Alfa One roger, I'll make it one-eighty.' There was a taut silence. I tried to imagine Arthur sitting there, on his own in an aeroplane which had come close to killing him. He would be suffering from shock, and I was far from convinced that he would use the approach speed I had given him, even after reading it back. 'Alfa One,' he called again, 'downwind checks complete.'

'Keep up the speed, Alfa One. Lose height in the turn, and make it a long, flat approach with plenty of power.'

'They're going to love him coming over nice and low,

piling on the power.' Jack Old indicated the eastern approach path, which lay over two villages.

'They'll have to lump it,' I said. 'At that speed, the approach path is flat in any case, and Arthur is in no state to make fine adjustments. I want him to drag it in with a lot of power to maintain height; that way, he has only to chop the throttles as he crosses the threshold and he's down.'

'Alfa One, turning finals, three greens.' Arthur sounded almost normal.

'Continue, Alfa One. Keep that speed up, use all the power you need. Tuck it well down for the last couple of miles.'

'Roger.' Arthur had the President lined up nicely, a fair way out. About six miles, I thought, two minutes yet to touchdown. I was becoming steadily more worried about how much fuel he had left, but I dared not ask him in case it made him panic again. There was, I reckoned, hardly enough to permit another circuit.

'That looks good, Alfa One.' The strain of extrapolating Arthur's approach was beginning to tell. If he allowed the speed to drop too low, he would need even more power to pull him out of trouble. I had encouraged him to lose height early, but he couldn't afford to lose too much, for the eastern end of the main runway—the last thousand feet or so—was built out on a shallow embankment, beyond which the approach lights rose on long stalks. 'Keep the speed at one-eighty,' I advised anxiously.

'Still one-eighty.' Arthur would know what he was in for by now. He was low enough to have a real impression of speed, something I had been denied during my landing by the darkness and the haze. In the cool clarity of the morning, Arthur would be all too conscious of the ground flashing beneath, and the runway looming ever closer. Without its flap blowing to add lift, the President was a hot ship: few aircraft, even military ones, aim to cross the hedge at two hundred miles an hour.

He was two miles out, no more, and still too high for my liking. 'Lower, Alfa One, lower.' I couldn't blame him for wanting the best possible view of the runway, but we couldn't afford an overshoot. It was some time since anyone in the tower had said anything; there was hardly any movement. Even Sir William stood rooted, his gaze fixed on the approaching aircraft.

'Hold the speed, Alfa One.' Something told me Arthur was getting nervous at his rate of progress. Obediently, the smoke from the engines thickened slightly. He still looked high to me. I framed my next piece of advice and thought better of it; at this stage, it wouldn't help Arthur to have me screaming in his ear. It was just as likely to put him off as to give him a better chance. Instead, I crossed my fingers firmly and watched, like everyone else.

Even from the tower, the approach seemed alarmingly fast. Arthur had fixed the speed in his mind and was determined to hold it. Only at the last moment did he throttle back, and not until then did he gain the confidence to drop the nose and aim for the runway threshold. The movement was too abrupt and he checked it sharply, which certainly cost him a few knots. The President ballooned, slowing even more, and then the nose dropped again. It touched, bounced, and swallowed a thousand feet of runway in a final ten-foot hop.

Arthur put a stop to that by selecting reverse thrust. There was no finesse about the way he did it, he simply banged the throttles wide open and the President slowed rapidly, nose well down. Then, suddenly, he almost lost it. One of the engines flamed out. His fuel was finished—it had been that close—and the port engine lost power before the starboard. At something like a hundred miles an hour the aircraft swung away from us. Arthur corrected as best he could, but was caught out again as the other engine flamed out in its turn. His desperate control movements must have used up what was left of the hydraulic pressure, but at least he kept it on the runway. With nothing but friction left to slow it, the President rolled on at decreasing speed far, far down the runway until eventually it rolled over the far threshold and came gently into contact with the first of the approach lights. It was immediately surrounded by emergency vehicles, and I felt a profound sense of anti-climax. There was a sense of relief in the control tower which one might almost have reached out and felt.

'It may not have been good,' I said, and I was conscious of the strain in my voice, 'but it was the best one so far. The next one should be all right.'

◢18◣

George should have been in hospital, but there was no question of that for the time being. Morlands' own medical staff had splinted the torn and broken thigh, and been duly warned to say nothing. His face was pale, and reflected a good deal of his agony.

'Make it easy,' I invited. 'Tell us where she is.'

'You, Goddard? After what you've done?' The sweat stood out on his forehead.

'Don't tempt me, George. I'm trying to forget what *you've* done. You're going to come out of this better than you deserve; nicely patched up and free to go. But you don't get any pain-killer until you've given me Liz.'

'Whistle for her, Goddard.' He actually smiled.

'George, don't be stupid,' I pleaded. 'The longer we leave your leg, the more difficult it will be to set.' It was on the tip of my tongue to tell him how little Liz meant to me—or did she? The last few hours had brought me so much closer to Jean, but would I change my mind when I saw Liz again? It was no good thinking that George might have done me a good turn by getting rid of her. She was being held somewhere, and we had to get her out.

'I'm going to limp for the rest of my life,' complained George.

'What do you want, Simpson?' Sir William Morland had

172

his anger on a tight rein. 'You know the position. We'll
look after you, right enough, but you'll lead us to Mrs
Goddard first. After that, we'll talk about the people behind you.'

'Will we? Maybe...'

I had a sudden feeling that George was playing for time.
Time to think, perhaps, or time for his confederates to
cover their tracks. For some of them, it was already too
late. We had missed the gunman at the mine entrance, he
must have realised something was amiss when the President had landed more or less normally. The other two,
however, whom Jean and I had locked in our former
prison, were safely held. In the end, of course, they would
go free. No scandal meant no police, and there was nothing
else to be done.

'Neil,' said Jean, 'how many people did George have
working for him?' She frowned at the figure on the couch.
'He wouldn't have hired more than he needed, would he?
I mean, he's too cautious a character to spread the risk
farther than necessary.'

'What do you mean?' I watched George rather than Jean,
and there was no doubt that he was paying her anxious
attention.

'Apart from George himself, how many men did we ever
see?'

'Only three.'

'Exactly. Suppose he didn't have any more?'

'What if he didn't?' I wished Jean would tell us plainly
what she meant.

'How would he have looked after Liz? Isn't it more
likely that she's somewhere in the same mine building?'

Perhaps the pain was too great to allow George his cus-
tomary measure of self-control, but I could have sworn he
relaxed. 'She's a bright girl, Goddard,' he said, 'but she
jumps to conclusions, doesn't she?'

'There you are!' exclaimed Jean. 'He's trying to put you
off. Surely it's worth *looking*? Neil, if he gets her away, our
hands will be tied **again**.'

'Not really. It's too late to crash the President now.'

'I know that. But he's thinking of the people at the

back of all this. If he can use Liz as a bargaining point...'

It made a certain amount of sense. George was sufficiently tenacious to bargain from any point of strength, though in this case it was difficult to see what he might hope to gain. His main aim was irretrievably lost, so his only object could be to protect his masters—out of loyalty, or possibly fear if they had blackmailed him into it. He must know that I already knew where to look for them, so any arrangement would depend on his accepting my word to say and do nothing in exchange for Liz. Either that, or George had a card up his sleeve about which I knew nothing.

'Sir William,' I said, 'did your works security people search the mine thoroughly, or did they simply bring out the two men we told them about?'

'They will have searched thoroughly.' George said it with a smile. 'I trained them; they will have done the job properly.'

'You know what, Goddard?' Morland's eyes had narrowed. 'I agree with Miss Partington. He's playing for time. Yonder mine's such a jumble of buildings you'd need an army to search it without missing anything. I've an idea we can do something about that.' He moved across to the telephone. 'We've people here who used to work in that mine before it closed. We'll get three or four of them together, and then we'll have a look.'

Jean looked pleased, but George glanced at the clock as though calculating some unseen margin.

Had I been able to think clearly, the whole thing would have been obvious even then. George had given me everything I needed to work it out, but I had been led astray by a plausible alternative. An hour later he practically spelled it out, but my mind was locked on the wrong course.

We had perforce to use the sick bay as our base of operations. My hope was still that George would crack under the constant pressure of pain, that we would be spared the trouble of a long and tedious search. By that time I was convinced that Jean was right, and Liz was incarcerated somewhere in the mine buildings.

The task of sorting out the ex-miners from Morlands'

work force, and selecting from them the few who would be at the same time the most useful and the least likely to talk afterwards, inevitably proved slow. George followed every move with interest—as a good security man, he probably knew most of the people concerned. He waited until four grim Yorkshiremen had been gathered, and then gracefully gave in.

'I think,' he said, 'that you might actually find Mrs Goddard, sooner or later. Shall we make it sooner? This leg of mine is beginning to play up a bit.'

'Just tell us where to look, George.'

'It's not as easy as that. The place is such a mess, it isn't a case of being able to give simple directions.'

'So what do you suggest?' It was almost as though he had changed his mind and elected to play for time once more.

'We'll get the whole thing over more quickly if I come along and show you.' He blinked, then stared at me, his mouth open. The vacancy of his expression spoke of a man wholly occupied with containing pain. George, I thought, was on the verge of cracking.

'Nothing doing, George.' Deliberately, I pushed him harder still. 'By the time we've found you a wheelchair and messed about loading you into a vehicle, we've lost another half-hour. If you ask me, you're after getting your pain-killer without giving anything in return.'

His eyes widened in anger, but only for a moment. 'Have it your own way. Without me, it will take you hours to find her.'

'He could be right, Neil.' Jean frowned at George. 'What do we lose by taking him along? Give him a local anaesthetic now, and take along the rest of the stuff so that we can put him to sleep when he's led us to Liz. If we don't find her soon, she's going to be pretty hungry.'

As usual, Jean made sense. I was doing Morlands' medical people less than justice in reckoning on half an hour. By the time the doctor had pumped George's thigh full of novocaine, they had found a collapsible wheelchair. We wheeled the patient out into the fresh air and installed him in a van, surrounded by our search party. Despite the injections the whole process must have pained him a good deal, but he went through it with jaw set and eyes constantly on the move. I knew I didn't trust him, even at this stage. But what could he do, crippled and alone? My main worry, however, was the reason why he had stalled us so long and then meekly given in. There was no answer I could think of.

We drove out through the main gate, and immediately turned sharp left into the mine entrance. A Morlands security man saluted Sir William, who sat beside the driver. The old man was determined to see the thing through, and in view of what was at stake I could hardly blame him. Jean was equally determined, and I had been able to suggest no good reason why she should stay behind. Apart from all else, she pleaded, it would be as well to have a woman on hand when we found Liz.

George gave his instructions clearly and firmly. Our four ex-miners held his wheelchair tightly in place in the back of the van, and would hoist him down when the time came.

'Left here,' he said, and we followed the main track between the towering slag heaps. The world of the airfield was already lost to us, though it was a matter of yards away. 'Bear right.' The track wound back the other way, and we found ourselves in the same dreary, empty yard into which Jean and I had emerged three hours previously. The shadows were shorter, but otherwise nothing had changed, except that the doors of the garage stood wide open. The towering hoists seemed even more forlorn than when we had climbed to their summit.

'In there.' George indicated the garage, and our driver took the van inside. So Jean had been right, I thought. They had been keeping Liz somewhere close to us, and all George's talk of hostages in separate places had been intended only to confuse and impress. I had certainly accepted it with far too little question.

We lifted George down from the van and placed him at the head of our procession, flanked by two of the former mineworkers whose combined task was to light the way and stop George if he tried to do anything silly. So far he hadn't put a foot wrong, but my nagging doubt persisted. He knew we could find this place, we hadn't needed him to show us; so why had he insisted on coming along? It seemed likely that if he had one final trick, we would see it within the next five minutes.

The lights flickered and probed their way along the corridor, throwing features into sharp relief.

'I thought the emergency lighting was supposed to be working, still?' The voice of one of the leading miners sounded refreshingly normal.

'It was,' I called, 'until we fused it. Why was it thought necessary, once the mine was closed?'

'There's still a bit of care and maintenance goes on,' explained one of the others. 'You've no idea what a labyrinth of tunnels runs under the moor, not only from this pit but all the others. Were one of the active pits to suffer a disaster, the best way in might easily be through here. That's why the main shaft is kept open.'

'Open? I didn't see it.'

'It was out there, none the less, under the winding gear tower. It's not much to look at, anyhow; after seeing all that machinery, you'd maybe expect to find a bloody great hole in the ground. It's big enough, I grant you, but it's bricked round to stop the local kids getting in and falling down the thing.'

'How far would they fall?'

'Best part of half a mile. Mind you, they'd hit t'walls on way down.' He relished his grim sense of humour. 'Like as not they'd be dead before they made their splash.'

'Splash?'

'Aye. Bottom of shaft is a drainage level, see? Always water down there, below the lowest active gallery.'

'What was this place?' I wanted to get him off his chosen subject.

'Storage for explosives and inflammables. They built it like a blockhouse in the early days, and let the slag spill over it to add even more strength. By the time they'd finished, you could have had an almighty bang in here without doing more than blowing t'doors off.'

We passed by the place where Jean and I had spent the last night, took a side corridor and then another. George still hadn't convinced me that his presence had helped us very much.

'You tucked her well away, didn't you?' I called.

'Principal guest, old boy. Couldn't have you hear her scream, could I?'

'She's not going to love you when she's let out, George. You'd better start feeling sorrier than that, or I might just stand by and watch while she scratches your eyes out.'

'You wouldn't do any such thing.' His confidence astonished me. 'You're far too soft-hearted, Goddard. It's sheer luck you didn't end up on the President casualty list; but everyone's luck runs out at some stage.' His voice echoed down the corridors. We had less room for manoeuvre in those nether regions, and I was even more on the alert.

'Stop here.' Long accustomed to command, George even now issued his orders curtly. He indicated a door on our left. 'Sort of guardhouse,' he said. 'You'll find a bunch of keys inside, hanging.'

It may well have amused him to see the way I went through the door, but I was past caring. Whatever I was thinking might be waiting in the room beyond, I was doomed to disappointment—or relief; nothing stirred as I kicked it open and dodged inside. There was nothing but a table, and a camp bed, a pack of cards and two candles in bottles. The keys hung on a nail on the wall.

'Carry on,' said George. 'One more turn to the left, ten feet, and stop at the door on the right.' The dust crunched under the wheels of his invalid chair. 'Shall I take the keys and open the door, Goddard? Or would you care to give us all another example of your ill-considered technique?'

His sneer passed me by, but he posed a serious question. Assuming his final trump card lay behind the door at which we had now arrived, would I do better to send him through first, or take a look myself?

Half my trouble was that I was thinking too hard to take account of the obvious: that was Jean's speciality. She eased past me, took the keys and gave them to George. 'Which one?' she said.

'I'm not sure.' He smiled up at her with a touch of defiance.

'Take your time,' said Jean. 'We'll find out what's in there before we do anything rash.' She thumped on the door, but there was silence. 'Liz,' she called, 'are you there?'

'Jean?' The small voice came from the far side. 'Is that you? What do they want us to do now?'

'It's all right, Liz.' Jean did her best to sound reassuring. 'We've come to get you out. It's all over, the President is safe and George Simpson can't harm you now.'

'What happened to him?'

'He's here,' said Jean. There was a muffled gasp from the far side of the door. 'It's all right,' she insisted. 'He's got a broken leg, and we're pushing him along in a wheelchair.'

'How did he break his leg?' Liz sounded a shade more confident, while George sorted slowly and deliberately through the bunch of keys.

'Neil shot him,' called Jean, and reduced Liz to silence.

'That one,' said George suddenly, handing it to Jean. She took it, entered it in the lock and turned. It was a long moment while she fumbled with the lock, then she turned the handle and the door swung open.

My suspicion of George evaporated. There was nothing inside the room except Liz, looking incredibly small and fragile as our lights caught her standing there. She threw a hand across her eyes as the beam of the lantern caught them. Her face was dirty, and her blonde hair hung in tangled streamers.

'Neil,' she said weakly, 'can I lean on you?'

'Come here,' I said, looking round for Jean. This was why she had come, but she was nowhere to be seen. The reflection of the lamplight from the dark walls showed only the circle of male faces. Even George's expression appeared to soften as Liz threw her arms round me and buried her face in my chest. We stood like that for some time, for I was unwilling to risk upsetting her. She needed time and gentleness if she was to recover.

'Oh, Neil!' Her voice came muffled from somewhere below my chin. 'Days, I've been here. I've never been so scared, and the worst thing of all was wondering what had happened to you.' She sobbed softly. 'Take me out, will you?' she pleaded. I grasped her by the shoulders and piloted her through the door and into the corridor. Her progress was slow and painful, and at one stage I thought I would have to carry her; either that, or haul George out of his wheelchair and come back for him later. Jean's absence puzzled me more and more, for she was hardly the type to break down and flee the sight of a touching reunion.

Liz breathed the fresh air as though it was an entirely new sensation for her. It seemed to lend her strength, and she stood back and looked at me. 'How are you, love?' she asked.,

'Fitter than you, I expect.' I tried to show concern and comfort at the same time.

'Jean said you shot George.' She sounded almost accusing.

'It was the only way I could stop him.'

'Anyway,' said Liz, 'where is Jean? She was there, wasn't she? Outside the place where they kept me, I mean.'

'Perhaps she wanted to fade into the background and leave us together.' It sounded stupid even as I said it, but what other explanation could there be?

'That's not like her. Didn't she say anything?'

'Not a word.'

'Oh, well.' A small frown creased Liz's brow. 'Where are the police?' she asked suddenly.

'They aren't.' The frown reappeared and I hastened to explain. 'It's all very complicated, Liz. We know more or less what happened, but it would be difficult to bring charges. If the whole affair was dragged into the open, it would reflect badly on the Ministry, and I doubt if it would do Morlands any good. And don't forget I shot George more or less in cold blood.'

'Yes,' she said thoughtfully. 'Yes, I see that.' She turned to gaze at George. 'What sort of state is he in now?'

'He'll live,' I said unfeelingly. 'His thigh is shot full of local anaesthetic, and we'll give him the rest of the works now he's fulfilled his side of the bargain.'

'You might as well, I suppose. You'll be able to use him, won't you, to put your case behind the scenes?'

It came as a considerable relief to see how rapidly Liz was regaining her balance. 'We'd be poorly placed without him,' I said. 'He was their chief of operations in the field, as it were; our only direct contact with those above.'

'But you know who they were? Didn't you tell me that young man at the Ministry had something to do with it? What will happen to him, do you think?'

'Well, nobody can afford to make a fuss. That goes for both sides. He'll be shunted off to some third-rate diplomatic post, to keep him well clear of mischief for the rest of his life. There's always the chance that some bunch of revolutionaries will see that justice is done one day. As for George, he'll be looked after. Morlands will pay the nursing home bill for putting his leg back together again, and I doubt if he'll starve in later life.' George was sitting patiently in his chair, and nobody was in much of a hurry to put him out of his misery. It astonished me that he was content to sit quietly. Had I been in his position, I would have been screaming for the promised injection the moment I had reached daylight.

'And there's really nothing more you can do?' asked Liz. 'Does poor John Rose have to go unavenged?'

'I'm afraid it looks like it. It's an unfair world, Liz.'

'It is,' she said. 'Sometimes, at any rate.' She hesitated, then seemed to sway and sag in the bright sunshine. I took a step forward and she clutched at me. 'I'm sorry, Neil.' Her smallest voice came from somewhere below. 'I'm being so silly, now it's all over. I shall be all right. Which is the way out?'

'Over there.' I turned and pointed.

'As long as I know,' she said coldly. Her voice was raised in power, and took on a new quality. 'Don't move, anybody, except to do as I tell you. There's no point in being heroic, you haven't got enough to lose.'

The world simply stopped. Morland, George, the men who had come with us, all froze into a tableau, but that was only part of it. The sheer shock of hearing one's wife say a thing like that is followed by a conviction of utter madness, and then the more rational feeling that she is mad. The whole twisted train of thought chased through my mind, and was brought to a halt by the grinding of a gun in the region of my kidneys.

'Liz, love.' I dared not move. She was highly strung at the best of times and if her finger was on the trigger and the safety catch off I could all too easily find myself crippled for life. 'It's all right now,' I said gently. 'It's all over, don't you understand? We can all go home now?'

'Seven years,' she hissed. 'Seven years you've treated me as though I were some half-witted slattern.' She was being a good deal less than fair, but I knew what she was driving at. 'You might at least change your tune now.'

'Elizabeth,' I tried again, 'did anyone tell you how to use that thing?'

'It has what they call a hair-trigger,' she said calmly, 'and the safety catch is off.' Duly warned, I forebore to labour the point. 'George!' called Liz sharply, 'just how bad do you feel?'

'Bloody.' He was too far gone in pain to feel triumph.

'I should hope so. You were supposed to do a better job than this.'

'He was, wasn't he? Whatever you do now, in the final analysis you've lost.' I rubbed it in, not knowing quite where the argument would lead. 'Take him away if you want to. The President programme will go ahead anyway, that's the main thing.'

'That it will.' Morland took his turn, sensing what I was trying to do. 'You may think you're protecting your friends, Mrs Goddard, but you could be wrong. I was going to use Simpson as my lever to get things done, and if he's taken away I'll have to find something else; a spot of compromise, a framed charge, anything that'll work.'

I had underestimated Liz for seven years, it was hardly surprising to find Morland falling into the same trap with only the briefest of meetings to guide him. The contempt in her voice was all too clear. 'Two can play at that game, Sir William. My advice is to leave well alone. After all, Neil explained so clearly how quiet you wanted this keeping.' The pressure on my back eased, and I risked turning. Liz had taken two steps backwards, out of grabbing range. The pistol was pointing unwaveringly at my stomach. Someone had taught her well, and she had no nerves at all. 'Don't move, Neil,' she warned. 'The rest of you, put George in that van, is that clear? Do it carefully, because my beloved husband is at risk if you try anything, and after all he's done for Morlands, that would hardly be fair, would it?'

They made to lift George, and he groaned. The sweat stood out on his face despite the chill of the morning. I hoped he was well on the way to catching pneumonia.

'Wait.' Her voice was cold and hard. 'I'm not having him moaning away behind me. Give him that injection, take him out of the chair and lay him in the back.'

'We can't do that, ma'am.' One of the Morlands men was moved to protest. 'He'll roll about in there, and it'll make a hell of a mess of his leg.'

'That's my worry. *He* won't be feeling anything.' She motioned with the gun. 'Get on with it.'

I marvelled that I could have lived with this creature for seven years and never once glimpsed this callous side of her character. They held George and made the injection ready. 'Of course, George,' I said cheerfully, 'the easiest way for her to make sure you never tell a soul is to dump you into a river while you're still doped unconscious.'

'So that somebody can find a body with a bullet hole in it?' Liz had been ready for that one. 'Listen to me, Neil. So far we've steered clear of murder—direct, incontestable murder; I'll try and keep it that way.' George relaxed as the drug took effect. 'I'm going to drive out of here,' she said, 'and you're not going to stop me.'

'If you feel so strongly about it, why don't you lock us away back there?' I pointed to the building from which we had emerged.

'Do you take me for a fool? Do you think I'd risk shepherding six men down dark corridors? George tried to embroider *his* scheme, and look what happened. I'll stick to what I'm sure will work, and this will work, Neil, won't it? Once I'm away from here, you stand no chance of finding me until I've cleared up the mess.'

I was only too willing to believe her. George must have known what would happen; all the time I thought he had been stalling for time to give someone a chance to make off with Liz, he had actually been giving her time to instal herself. I had no doubt she had a confederate waiting with a car somewhere close at hand.

'Why should I stop you?' I said bitterly. 'Goodbye, Liz.' At least, I thought, something had come up on the credit side as far as I was concerned.

'Not goodbye, Neil.' I hoped it was just chance and not clairvoyance. 'We'll meet again, when all the fuss has died down. I shall pull my strings, and Sir William will pull his, and when the whole thing is tangled beyond redemption we can return to a life of domestic bliss, watching one another.' She even smiled, and the thought of it made my blood run cold. 'You wouldn't want any of this to come out, would you, Neil? You'll come back to me, and in future you'll treat me with the respect I deserve.'

The opening didn't even tempt me. I stood while she climbed into the van and started up, the gun still covering the whole group of us as we stood well clear. Morland and I both knew she held all the cards. She was making off with our only real evidence in the form of George Simpson, asleep in the back and strapped in as best they could manage. We dared not try and catch her, even less make a move against her in the days to come. At best she would head us off, at worst retaliate by leaking her version of the whole affair where it would do most harm. As for me, I was convinced she had given me fair warning that she wanted me back on her own terms. How long could she last before I wrung her neck, did she think?

The van slowly gathered way and turned to face the way out. We stood helpless as it picked up speed, heading past the big winding machinery tower for the gap between the slag heaps. In a few seconds it would be lost from view.

The whiplash crack startled the morning, and the van shied in sympathy. Again the sound came, and again; now the van was out of control, swinging in a great arc round the dusty yard. It described very nearly a complete circle, and ran into the machinery tower. I waited for the crunch of metal, but it missed the great steel pillars and vanished into the deep shadow. The noise which came was not at all the one I expected, but rather a dull thud and a silence. One

of the men swore and started forward, breaking the spell
for the rest of us. As we neared the tower the shadow resolved itself into more pillars and ladders and chains, and
amid them a wall of rough brick in which the van had
punched its hole. Even as we ran we heard the squeal and
clangour seemingly echoing through the ground, and finally,
after an appallingly long time, the splash.

There, too, deep in the shadow, we found Jean, sobbing
fiercely with a faraway look in her eyes.

# ◢19◣

'You *do* understand that the implications of this thing are
*very* far-reaching?'

'Yes, Minister.' It wasn't the first time I had met Sir
Barrington Mayhew, but in a manner of speaking it was the
first time he had met me. That is, he was very much aware
of me and at pains to make his point.

'The Director of Public Prosecutions maintained a very
open mind...'

'That's his job.' Reverence had never been my strong
point and circumstances made it even less so.

'...and his report was considered at great length by the
Cabinet.'

'I'll bet.'

'I beg your pardon?'

'Nothing, Minister.' In view of how well things were
turning out, I ought not to spoil them. It still intrigued
me how they were going to cover up the whole thing.
'Presumably the Cabinet reached some conclusion?' I encouraged him.

'They did, and a very logical one it was. We have a situation where it is very difficult to decide at what point the law was broken...'

'You surprise me, Minister.'

'No I don't, not in the least.' He pulled me up sharply. I was allowing flippancy to obscure the fact that Mayhew was as intelligent as he was pragmatic. 'You must have given the matter more thought than anyone,' he went on. '*Could* a prosecutor have turned anything that happened into a watertight case of murder, or even manslaughter? It's not certain. You seem to have sinned every bit as much as you were sinned against.'

'That's very uncharitable.' I was half-serious, unsure what line he would take.

'I'm not here to be charitable, Goddard,' he snapped. 'I'm here to serve the best interests of the country. It seems to me that some of those principally concerned are beyond any interest, while it remains for certain others to be convinced of the wisdom of silence and inactivity. Among those others, I include you.' He raised a hand to cut off my protest. 'The Ministries concerned, as well as Morland Aircraft, feel the whole thing is best laid to rest.'

'Suppose somebody comes from outside and digs for it?'

'Why would they do that? And where, pray, would they dig?' He blinked across his desk. 'Full knowledge of what happened is confined to a very exclusive circle, of which you happen to be a member.'

'Yes, sir.' I felt it was high time to be dutiful.

'I have here,' he said, shuffling a collection of files, 'an official account of what took place. It takes account of everything, and leaves no loopholes. You will read it,' he said, 'and then read it again, and work away at it until it seems more real than the reality. It's not for release,' he stressed. 'It's not for use at all unless anyone comes *digging*, as you put it.' He wrinkled his nose. 'Then we'll have to say look here, it's no good smelling a story, this is all that happened, what?'

'Yes, indeed, sir.'

'Yes, indeed. But it had better be consistent as well as blameless, so learn it.'

'There is one other thing, sir.' I had a feeling he was waiting for me to raise the point.

'What is that?' He sat back expectantly.

'Miss Partington.'

'My dear boy,' he smiled, 'I'm quite sure you're capable of taking care of that little problem without our having to spell it out to you.'

Perhaps; but I didn't altogether share his confidence.

After all that had gone before, the two inquests, on John and his crew and on Liz and George, were something of an anticlimax. The old coroner took it entirely seriously, and so I suppose did everyone else, in their own way. I couldn't even work out who was simply acting, and who accepted the explanations as the truth.

It was, in any case, stretching a point to call them explanations; presumptions would have been more like it. In John's case, the jury brought in a verdict of accidental death with a rider about more frequent medical checks for industry test pilots. They accepted the demise of Liz and George with less interest, complaining that far too many people were able to wander round disused mine workings, and that the Coal Board should devise a better way of sealing former shafts. With that, we all filed out into the December sunshine, and the first—the only—person I saw was Jean.

She was an issue I had been avoiding, in the fear that anything she had to do with me might open the flood-gates of memory. It is one thing to have good self-control, and another to send two people crashing down a mine shaft, however unintentionally.

'Hallo, Neil.' She looked at me almost anxiously.

'Hallo, Jean. How are you?' It stumbled out too fast. People brushed past us unnoticed. The Barnsdale shops were full of Christmas cheer.

'It's not such a bad place, is it?' she said gently, and reached for my hand. 'You don't have to worry about me, you know.'

'Are you sure?'

'Of course I'm sure. You know what upset me, that day?

That it was all over, that the pressure was off; that we'd no more reason to be together.'

'And that you knew the best story of your career would never see the light of day.'

'That's where you came in, Neil Goddard.' She laughed. 'Do you want to try starting again?'

'Not for a bit, thanks.' What manner of invitation was that? 'Jean,' I asked, 'what put you on to Liz? You spotted something, didn't you?'

'Lots of little things,' she said, and her eyes went out of focus for a moment as though she were stringing them together on a mental thread. 'She suddenly appeared up here when you were starting to make progress, didn't she? And she knew that man from your Ministry, who's been posted to the Congo or somewhere. She didn't even bother to hide it from you.'

'She said I'd introduced them, even.'

'Maybe you did, at that. Anyway, my guess is that they found themselves quite well suited: he wanted her money. She wanted someone who'd do as he was told.' She hesitated. 'Poor Neil,' she said, 'does it hurt very much?'

'Only when I laugh.'

'I expect she strung him along, because she was like that. Then he and his friend from the Ministry of Defence...'

'The old school chum?'

'Exactly.' We strolled aimlessly away from the town centre, towards Barnsdale Park. 'Somehow,' ventured Jean, 'they dreamed up this lovely idea for achieving honour, glory and promotion. One wanted to do it for his father, who was suffering weekly apoplexy at the thought of Morlands selling aeroplanes to the wrong people, and the other wanted to do it for Liz.'

'What would he have done about me?'

'Neil, love, that's why they went to such lengths to get you up here. They thought first of all that you wouldn't do a very good job, second that Liz would be able to head you off if you did get anywhere, and third that the chance might come up to get rid of you altogether.'

'They must have been pleased to see me fly the President with Arthur Morland.'

'They did better than that, I know for a fact. Did you know George Simpson actually fed Sir John Lovegrove the idea that you were running specific tests for explosive traces? It was a miracle Lovegrove's people didn't do away with you there and then.'

'Who told you that?'

'My father. Don't forget he knows a good deal of what went on at the time. You needn't worry about him, he wants to see Morlands stay in business more than anyone; but he told me how Lovegrove came worrying round Number Five the day after you vanished. He heard Simpson explaining how careful they had to be, because of the tests that were being run. It worried dad, for he knew they were trying to keep everything quiet, but Lovegrove was a director so he accepted it at the time.'

'My dear wife knew what was going on the whole time? Do you really believe that?'

'I'm afraid so, Neil. Not just knew, but organised. From her point of view it was a chance to get her own back on you, and lay hands on a man who would be more than amenable, because she'd have had a blackmail hold over him. He'd have had to crawl for the rest of his life.'

'She did point something of the sort out to me,' I confessed, 'just before...'

'You never took her seriously, Neil.' Jean skilfully altered course before the pause could become a silence. 'You rode roughshod over all her schemes and there was nothing she could do, until this chance appeared out of the blue.'

'I see that now, Jean. But you couldn't have known at the time: how did she give herself away?'

'I was with her when you flew the President, remember? When we saw it take off, I thought I was in trouble, for I knew Liz was intelligent enough to put two and two together. Yet she stayed very calm, as though nothing had happened. When we got back to the flat, though, and found them waiting, she made the devil of a fuss, and they took her off quickly. With the benefit of hindsight, it was too much of a contrast.'

'Hardly proof, though.'

'Agreed. That didn't come until we were back in the mine building. George gave me the key, did he not, and I opened the door?'

'So?'

'It wasn't locked.'

'Then why in hell didn't you say so?'

'Because I still wasn't sure, Neil.' Jean was on the defensive. 'She might simply have failed to realise it was open, or been too scared to come out. Otherwise, there was only one explanation, and I hadn't the time to work it out. I had to make sure.'

'How did you do that?'

'I just looked at her.' Jean saw I was groping for an answer. 'She was wearing a different frock,' she explained. 'She'd taken nothing with her, yet she'd changed.'

'Come, now,' I protested, 'they might have brought her something else to wear.'

'They wouldn't do it for me.' She let that ultimate argument sink in. 'But you see my position? You hardly believe me now, you surely wouldn't have done so then. Had I started to explain, she would have shown her hand much earlier, that's all. So I faded into the background and made my way outside, looking for some cover. I still hoped I was wrong, but if I wasn't, I had the gun.'

'Yes; the gun. Where did you find *that*?'

'I searched the second of our two warders, the one you never looked at.'

'You might have told me, love.'

'I was going to, but there didn't seem time. Anyway, you had one of your own.'

I thought there was more to it than that, but I doubted if Jean would ever admit it. 'Where is the gun now?' I asked.

'At the bottom of the mine shaft,' she said. 'Where else?'

I knew then that Jean had made a better recovery than me.


'I gather you've had a long chat with Barry Mayhew.'

There was comfort in the fact that Sir William Morland

was still on such terms with the Minister. 'That's right,' I said baldly.

'What did you talk about?'

'It was quite a wide-ranging discussion.' I fenced, not knowing how much even Sir William knew of our final arrangements.

'Did he mention that you were fired?'

The abruptness of it took me by surprise. 'He did not.'

'No? Well, we sort of split the job between us.' It was evident that Sir William knew everything. 'After what happened, he's of the opinion that you'd not feel too comfortable in the Ministry.'

'He's probably right, at that.'

'That being so,' he rumbled on, 'I'm offering you a position here: Chief Test Pilot.'

'What about Arthur?' I hated myself for having to ask.

'Arthur is on a world tour, at my expense. When he comes back, he'll do as he's told. He could learn a lot from you.'

'I'm flattered.'

'Are you so?' Sir William gathered himself for a second revelation. 'I'm also to offer you a directorship in Morlands.'

'That's a funny way to put it. As though it wasn't your idea.'

'It wasn't, though I might have come round to it in time. It's what you might call a package deal, Goddard. The Ministry wants to see the back of you, and we're prepared—nay, let's be honest, we're happy to take you. But the Ministry also wants us to behave better, so it wants you on the board. You'll owe the job to the Ministry, so you'll tend to represent their interests. You'll also be much less inclined to squawk, not that I think you would. It's just that they like to cover themselves all ways, these politicians.'

'I see.' It was tortuous reasoning, worthy of a top political mind. Of that there was no doubt.

'You don't see everything,' he warned.

'There's more?'

'One more item in the package, take all or leave all.' The pale blue eyes assumed a sparkle.

'And what's that?'

'Partington's daughter. Nice girl, that.'
'That's what I think.'
'Well, then, lad. *Do* something about it.'

So I did.